Cade cut Lyn off with a wave of his hand. "Forget it. I've heard it all before, and I doubt you have anything new to add that'll make a difference to me."

"Have it your way." With a simple shrug, she kept walking. No argument. No blustering anger. She seemed easygoing and laid-back. Disarming in her candor. And he couldn't help wondering about her ideas. For the first time, he really wanted to know. But asking her to explain seemed a bit like admitting defeat right now.

They soon arrived at her truck, her boots and pant legs covered by a thin sheen of dust. As she unlocked and opened the door to the driver's seat, she tilted her head to look up at him. "We might have conflicting opinions, Cade, but I can make a big difference here in Stokely. And I intend to do just that."

She climbed inside and reached for the armrest to pull the door closed. Before she did so, she gave him a smile so bright that it made his jaw ache.

Books by Leigh Bale

Love Inspired

The Healing Place
The Forever Family
The Road to Forgiveness
The Forest Ranger's Promise
The Forest Ranger's Husband
The Forest Ranger's Child
Falling for the Forest Ranger
Healing the Forest Ranger

LEIGH BALE

is an author of inspirational romance who has won multiple awards for her work, including the prestigious Golden Heart. She is the daughter of a retired U.S. forest ranger, holds a B.A. in history with distinction and is a member of Phi Kappa Phi Honor Society. She loves working, writing, grandkids, spending time with family, weeding the garden with her dog, Sophie, and watching the little sagebrush lizards that live in her rock flower beds. She has two married children and lives in Nevada with her professor husband of thirty-one years. Visit her website at www.LeighBale.com.

Healing the
Forest Ranger

Leigh Bale

HARLEQUIN® LOVE INSPIRED®

Recycling programs
for this product may
not exist in your area.

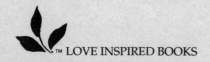 ™ LOVE INSPIRED BOOKS

ISBN-13: 978-0-373-81693-4

HEALING THE FOREST RANGER

www.LoveInspiredBooks.com

Printed in U.S.A.

God hath not given us the spirit of fear; but of power, and love, and of a sound mind.
—*2 Timothy* 1:7

For Wilma Counts, a dear friend and confidante.
Super woman in disguise.
And a great author in her own right.

And many thanks to the U.S. Forest Service
and the Bureau of Land Management for the
tremendous work they do in conserving our national
resources. Our natural resources would be in a
huge mess if it weren't for these highly trained and
experienced professionals. They're ordinary people
with a gargantuan and sometimes impossible job
to do. We're lucky to have them.

Thanks also to Sara Goldberg,
a prosthetist with Hanger Clinic.
Her kindness in answering my questions
about prosthetics and amputees saved me from
embarrassment. Thanks for taking precious time out
of your busy day to help me, Sara. You rock!

And much gratitude to Rachel Burkot for lifting my
spirits sky-high when I was at the lowest of lows.
And you did it without even knowing what it meant
to me. I appreciate you. More than I can ever say.

Note: Any errors or opinions in this book are mine
alone and not meant to offend anyone in any way.

Chapter One

They didn't know she was watching. Lyndsy Warner crouched low behind a rock outcropping. Prickles of excitement dotted her arms. She held her breath, hoping the wild horses wouldn't catch her scent and bolt. At least not yet.

Overhead, a hawk spiraled through the azure sky. The late April weather had been unseasonably warm. Tufts of green grass and red paintbrush trembled as the breeze whispered past, carrying the earthy smell of dust and sage.

Letting her camera hang limp from the strap around her neck, Lyn reached up to remove the bronze shield pinned above the right front pocket of her forest ranger's shirt. A glint from the afternoon sun might give her presence away to the mustangs in the valley below.

After tucking the badge into her pants pocket, Lyn reached for the camera again. Holding it up to her eyes, she adjusted the focus and studied the herd through the lens. Five mustangs, led by a handsome buckskin stallion. The stud's black mane and tail stood out against his golden coat. The band included three mares and a black foal with a white tail and mane. Not really black, but almost, with just a bit of white on her hind left foot and on her right, under the flank and in her mane and tail. Not a true pinto, either. Very unique coloring and absolutely stunning. The filly's spindly legs looked long and strong, a foreshadowing of the beautiful mare she'd become. Wild and free.

Lyn snapped a quick series of pictures, wishing she could share this moment with Kristen, her ten-year-old daughter. Like most girls, Kristen loved horses. But these mustangs carried a deeper meaning for Lyn—a reminder of the night her husband died.

The bony rib cages of the horses seemed too lean, an indicator of sparse forage on the range. As the herds increased, there just wasn't enough for them to eat, not to mention the other wildlife roaming this area, or the beef cattle the ranchers paid the government to graze.

Lyn zoned in on the stallion she'd named Buck. This wasn't the only herd foraging in Secret Valley. Lyn had named all the stallions living among the mountains of McClellan National Forest, but not their mares and foals. She didn't want to become more attached to them than she already was. Especially if she was forced to round up some of them for removal.

A low nicker drew Lyn's attention to the plateau overhead. A smaller dun stallion stood gazing down upon the tranquil family of mustangs, his cream coloring similar to Buck's except that tiger stripes circled his front legs. A throwback from prehistoric horses. Probably a bachelor stallion, with no mares of his own. His ears pricked forward with rapt attention, and Lyn knew he wanted Buck's mares. Or at least one of them.

"Don't do it, buddy. Buck's a lot bigger, and he'll hurt you if you try to steal one of his girls." The warm breeze stole Lyn's whispered warning.

While Buck's lead mare kept watch, two of the other mares dipped their noses into the murky water of the shallow spring. No vegetation grew here, with the banks beaten down and churned to mud by too many tromping hooves. By mid-May, Lyn figured the water would be gone. Dried by the baking sun to nothing but cracked earth. The horses needed this water. Desperately. Without it, they'd have to journey across the mountains to Cherry Creek, a thin stream nine miles away. An arduous trip that would sap their energy, keep them from feeding, and weaken their foals.

Always on the lookout, Buck noticed the bachelor stallion and snorted. He skirted the edge of his band, tossing his proud head and pawing the dirt with one hoof. With his long tail flying high like a flag, he raced toward the plateau, placing himself between the watering hole and the bachelor. Buck wouldn't give up his mares. Not without a fight.

The dun neighed in challenge, then picked his way down the steep grade. As he reached the valley floor, he lifted his elegant head and arched his muscular neck. A dark dorsal stripe ran down the middle of his back, and Lyn decided to name him Stripe.

Absolutely gorgeous.

Buck didn't think so. He let out a shrill squeal. Ears flat against his head, he raced toward the dun. At first, the two stallions circled one another, snorting and sizing each other up.

Stripe ducked away from Buck and chased after a plump dapple-gray mare that looked ready to foal soon. Stripe nudged her rump, urging her forward, trying to whisk her away. Buck intercepted, biting Stripe's hindquarters. The mare knew who she belonged to and lashed out at Stripe with her hind legs. Buck bared his teeth, the whites of his eyes showing. His black mane whipped across his strong neck like billows of smoke.

Stripe circled back, chasing after the mare, desperate for a mate. Buck followed, neighing his disapproval. The bachelor stallion was lean and tough, but no match for the more experienced buckskin.

And the battle began.

Both stallions reared. Screaming, biting, slashing each other with their razor-sharp hooves. Again and again, their hooves thudded against each other like iron clubs. Lyn cringed at the horrific noise they made. Survival of the fittest. Their ferocity frightened her on a primitive level. She lowered her camera and stared in shock.

The mares galloped out of the fray, the black foal scurrying to join the safety of her mother. Stripe followed, still trying to separate the dapple-gray from the rest of the herd.

Buck intervened with a roar of rage. He kicked— once, twice, bludgeoning Stripe in the head and shoulder. The bachelor stallion staggered and dropped to his front knees. Buck offered no mercy. Rearing, he came down hard on top of Stripe's head.

Lyn gasped, remembered her camera and started clicking again. Later on, the unique photos would serve as an amazing record of wild-horse behavior.

Stripe screeched in pain. Buck gave the younger stallion just a moment to recover his feet. With a loud grunt, the beaten horse sprinted toward the safety of the mountains. He'd been whipped and gave up the fight for now, but Lyn knew he'd return later for another try. The urge to have a family was as old as time, something instilled in the majority of God's creatures. And one day Stripe, or another stronger stallion, would defeat Buck. But for now, the older stallion had kept his harem intact. In this small corner of the world, he reigned supreme.

Buck trotted around the perimeter of the watering hole, head up and nostrils flared as he watched for the return of the dun. Still wound up. Still angry. Unwilling to accept any nonsense right now.

And that's when Lyn saw the blood running down Buck's right front leg. She focused the camera, trying to see the wound more clearly, but no good. She had to get closer.

Moving silently down the hill, she skimmed through snags of PJ's, short for piñon-junipers. She stayed upwind, hoping to go undetected by the band of horses. As she inhaled the dry desert air, her booted feet sank deep into the sunbaked sand. And that was her first mistake.

She stumbled, twisting her ankle. She stifled the cry rushing up her throat, but her silence made no difference. The agitated stallion lifted his head and looked her way. Still territorial and furious. Still ready to fight.

With a scream of fury, Buck charged.

Lyn's breath froze in her throat. A bristle of panic raced down her spine. She glanced over her shoulder. No use trying to reach her truck. There wasn't time.

Instead, she ducked under a thicket of PJ's and pressed her body back into the prickly trees. Sharp needles scratched her hands and face. Her fear overshadowed the pain. The stallion screamed again, thrashing toward her, ferocious and enraged.

Lyn's flesh burned with alarm. Her heart beat madly in her chest. She was no match against the horse's battering hooves. He'd kill her if he could.

Buck reared, hooves waving dangerously near Lyn's head. She scrunched farther back into the crowded trees. The hair of her long ponytail ripped against the pointed branches.

One thought pounded in her brain. Kristen. All alone in the world. If Lyn were killed, her little daughter would have no one to love and care for her. No one to keep her safe.

The rearing mustang beat the PJ's to splinters, fiercely determined to reach her.

Lyn screamed in helpless anguish. How had this happened? A calm afternoon of checking the watering hole had turned into a life-threatening situation.

Lyn glanced left and right, desperate for a safer place to hide until the stallion gave up and left. A thick outcropping of sage and PJ's jutted from the rocks just to her right. To reach it, she'd have to leave her fragile sanctuary and run for her life. With a crazed beast hot on her tail.

Bracing her hands beneath her in the dirt, Lyn bent down like a track star, knowing there was absolutely no way she could outrun this horse. Knowing she might be killed.

Taking a deep breath, she sprinted toward the rocks.

The wild horses were fighting. Caden Baldwin recognized their screams echoing through the canyon, reaching his ranch a mere six miles outside the town of Stokely, Nevada. Riding Flash, his bay gelding, Cade galloped toward Secret Valley. Maybe he'd get to see his beloved mustangs today. He couldn't remember a single summer in his childhood when he hadn't watched the wild horses with his grandfather. It'd been several weeks since they'd crossed Cade's pasture land and—

A woman's scream echoed off the rock walls of the ravine like a gunshot. What on earth?

Cade tapped his heels against his horse's sides. Flash tore off at a fast run. Someone was in trouble. Someone needed help.

And then the panic set in. So unexpected that it left Cade breathless and choking. He clung to the saddle, overwhelmed by a flashback to the war in Afghanistan. The drumming of the horse's hooves became the pounding of gunfire and shells exploding all around Cade, hammering his body with bits of rock, dirt and mortar. The memory of pain and the metallic taste of blood in his mouth seemed so real. And then a vision of Dallin filled his mind, his best friend's body, limp and bleeding. Broken.

Cade shook his head, trying to clear his mind and return to the present. Trying urgently to forget the haunting nightmare. He wasn't in the Middle East now. He was here in the Nevada desert. God had brought him home.

Safe and sound.

Oblivious of Cade's moment of crisis, Flash didn't break stride. Cade sat frozen in the saddle, his body moving with the strong rhythm of the horse. He clenched the reins, his calves tightening around the animal's sides.

As the wild mustangs came into view, Cade recovered his senses and his breathing slowed a bit. His gaze centered on a buckskin stallion rearing and thrashing through the pinions. A woman fought her way through the brush, frantically seeking cover. Chased by the stallion.

Urging Flash toward the wild mustang, Cade yelled and waved his arms. The lead mare neighed to the rest of her herd. From his peripheral vision, Cade saw her racing toward the sheltering mountains, the other mares and a young black foal following in hot pursuit.

The stallion snorted, shook his splendid head and chased after his band. Puffs of dust and flying clods of dirt marked their passing. Flash came to a halt, his sides heaving. Cade patted the gelding's neck, murmuring a soothing word to the breathless horse. Then he looked at the woman...and groaned. In an instant, Cade recognized the drab olive color of her shirt and spruce-green pants.

Forest Service.

He'd rescued a government employee. One of those people who wanted to move the wild horses off this land and lock them away in holding pens.

Cade had half a mind to turn around and ride back to Sunrise Ranch. The last person he wanted to help was a Forest Service worker. But he figured he should at least find out if she was all right. Since returning from the war, he had enough deaths on his conscience and didn't want to add another.

"You okay, lady?" he called.

She sat scrunched back within one of the taller pinions, trying to climb the slim tree trunk. As she descended from her perch, a sprinkle of gray-green nettles showered her head. The limb broke off, and she landed on her rump in the dirt. She gasped but came quickly to her feet, limping slightly. She brushed at her long ponytail and clothing before answering in a shaky voice. "Y-yes, I'm fine, thanks to you."

Honey-brown eyes. Beautiful, intelligent and filled with relief.

Cade pursed his lips and looked around for her vehicle. He saw nothing but scrubby sage and rabbit brush. "How'd you get out here?"

She pointed to the north. "My truck is parked beside the dirt road about a mile away."

He jerked his gaze in that direction. Just great. He'd have to give her a ride.

"You ready to go home now, or would you rather have more fun upsetting the mustangs?" He couldn't keep an edge of annoyance from his tone. He was sick and tired of government employees rounding up the wild horses to send them to holding stations where most of them lived their life in captivity. He'd never been overly sentimental, but he wanted to forget what he'd seen and been forced to do as a U.S. marine in a war zone. The wild-horse herds soothed his jangled nerves and helped him cope with his post-traumatic stress disorder.

The mustangs were Cade's version of therapy.

The woman showed a weak smile, her eyes sparkling like amber gems. Streaks of dirt marred the smooth curve of her sunburned cheeks. Pine needles and dirt clung to her long, white-blond ponytail. A smattering of freckles across the bridge of her nose indicated she spent a lot of time outdoors. Because of her employment, Cade decided right then and there he wouldn't like her one bit. No sirree. Not as long as she posed a threat to his wild horses.

She pointed toward the mountains. "That stallion is injured. He fought with a bachelor, and I was trying to get a closer look to see how bad the wound might be."

Her declaration surprised him. Since when did a Forest Service employee care if a wild stallion was wounded or not?

"The way he hightailed it out of here, I'd say he'll be just fine," Cade said. "It's not wise to come out here and gawk at the mustangs. They can be very dangerous."

Her pink lips tightened defensively. "I wasn't gawking. I was checking water levels and observing the horses, trying to learn their habits and see how well fed they are."

He bit the inside of his cheek to keep from laughing. "You can call it whatever you like. It's the same thing."

"I wasn't gawking," she insisted.

Okay, he wouldn't argue with her about it. "So, how'd it all work out for you?"

She didn't seem to catch his humor.

"They saw me when I changed position." A frown of disappointment creased her forehead.

"As if a wild stallion would ever let you get close enough to offer first aid." Cade muttered the words beneath his breath. What was she thinking? A mustang would never let her walk up to him and bandage his injured leg.

Her expression darkened. "I know that. I just wanted to see if he needed help."

"Do you come out here often?" Cade asked.

Her gaze met his without flinching. "Every Friday, when I have the time. But not just here in Secret Valley. I make excursions to several areas, checking the water sources in the mountains and valleys. Quite frequently, I come upon the horses. What's your name?"

Cade stared at the Forest Service woman for several moments, mesmerized by her commanding presence in spite of her short height and slim build. Not many people would get this close to a wild horse. Most stallions, even the tame ones, were fierce and treacherous. This woman had grit, he'd give her that. Or perhaps she was too foolish to realize the danger she'd been in. Another city girl who didn't realize that wild horses were wild.

"Most people call me Cade." He rested his arms across the saddle horn and leaned forward.

She paused as though waiting for him to ask her name. But honestly, he didn't want to know any more about her. In the ensuing silence that followed, Flash flicked his tail at a fly.

"Are you from around here?" she asked.

Cade jerked his thumb up. "I own a small ranch just west of here."

"Ah, Sunrise Ranch." She nodded.

He wasn't surprised she knew his place. The community wasn't large, and everyone knew everyone else. So, why hadn't he met this woman before? He longed to ask where she'd come from, but resisted the urge to show any interest.

"My name is Lyn," she said. "I'm fairly new in town. Only been here two months, so I haven't had an opportunity to meet you yet."

"Yeah. Come on. I'll take you to your truck." He removed his foot from the left stirrup and reached out a hand to help her step up behind him on his horse. His mind kept repeating her name. Lyn. It suited her—feminine yet decisive.

"No, thanks. I can walk."

She limped away, and he watched her with a bit of doubt. Maybe it was for the best. It wouldn't bode well if someone saw him riding with a Forest Service employee. He'd never hear the end of it. Instead, he rode along beside her, just in case she changed her mind.

"Did you hurt yourself?" He jutted his chin toward her left ankle.

"Just a sprain. I was out here checking the damage to the watering hole when I saw the horses. I didn't expect Buck to attack me. I'm sure he was still feeling defensive after his fight with the bachelor stallion. Otherwise, I doubt he would have bothered with me."

"Buck?"

"Yeah, that's what I named the buckskin."

Cade's jaw went slack, but he quickly turned his

face away so she wouldn't see his surprise. "You actually named one of the stallions?"

"Uh-huh. I take pictures of all the wildlife I see out here on the Stokely Ranger District." She explained about naming the stallions of each herd so she could keep track of them in her reports.

"Wait a minute. You're the new forest ranger?" He'd heard they were getting a new ranger in town, but had no idea she'd be a woman, or that she'd care about the wildlife enough to document them.

"That's right." She nodded and smiled pleasantly.

"Hmm."

"You don't sound pleased."

"I'm just indifferent." And stunned. A petite, attractive woman wasn't his idea of what a forest ranger ought to look like. In fact, he'd never met a woman ranger before. Especially not one this pretty. Most of the rangers he'd met were men with pot guts. Overbellies who wouldn't listen to reason. At least not where the wild horses were concerned. Cade wasn't sure what to think about this turn of events.

"I suppose you're planning to round up the wild horses and take them off the range," he grumbled.

"Not if I can help it." She kept her gaze trained on the rocky ground in front of her.

"What do you mean?"

"I love the wild horses. But I also love the elk,

antelope, bighorn sheep and mule deer. And they need to eat and drink out here, too."

"There's plenty of feed for all the wildlife," he said.

She stopped and looked at him squarely, resting her hands on her slim hips. A blaze of fire sparked in her eyes. As stunning as the wild mustangs he'd seen minutes earlier. "No, there's not. Buck's herd is starving. They're too lean—I could see that with my own eyes. And they'll soon be out of water."

What she said went against everything Cade had been brought up to believe in. "Bah! The mustangs have been running wild across this land for centuries. They'll make do. They always survive."

"Yes, but many will die a slow, cruel death. A lot of elk and deer will suffer the same fate. There isn't enough water and feed out here to sustain so many wildlife and domestic livestock, too."

He waved a hand. "You're just another cow lover. Get rid of all the ranchers' fat cattle, and the wildlife will have enough feed to live on."

She chuckled, not seeming offended in the least. "Well, I do enjoy eating a nice steak and hamburger now and then. But the ranchers are definitely restricted on how many cattle they can graze on public lands. They don't take more than their fair share, believe me. I won't let them."

That was just the problem. He didn't believe her.

"Ma'am, there are more important things out here than the ranchers and their cattle."

She brushed her hand across some sage. "There are miles of sagebrush out here. It's edible, but provides very little nourishment for the horses. They need grass. Wild horses don't migrate to better areas when food and water runs out. They just stay here and starve. And please, call me Lyn."

Not if he could help it.

She poked a tuft of Great Basin wheatgrass with the tip of her scuffed boot. "It takes fifty acres of this kind of land to feed one horse for one month. That doesn't include elk and mule deer, nor any cattle, either. You can do the math as easily as I can to figure out how many miles of land are needed to keep that wild-horse herd happy and healthy. But I can tell you this area can sustain about one hundred and fifty wild horses. We currently have over four hundred and fifty horses living in and around this national forest. And that's too many if we don't want to see them starve to death."

She turned and continued walking. In spite of his desire not to, he found himself liking the jaunty bounce of her hair. Spunky and sure of herself. He'd never met anyone like her.

He flinched when she whirled around and continued her dialogue.

"And you're wrong about the cattle. They're just as important as the wild horses. Every man, woman and child in this country needs to eat. And cattlemen make their living by growing cows. The horses are important. The cows are important. And so is the other wildlife out here. The issues aren't easy, but we need to find ways to make it all work together. And I have some ideas, if you'd like to hear them…"

He cut her off with a wave of his hand. "Forget it. I've heard it all before, and I doubt you have anything new to add that'll make a difference to me."

"Have it your way." With a simple shrug, she kept walking. No argument. No blustering anger. She seemed easygoing and laid-back. Disarming in her candor. And he couldn't help wondering about her ideas. For the first time, he really wanted to know. But asking her to explain seemed a bit like admitting defeat right now.

They soon arrived at her truck, her boots and pant legs covered by a thin sheen of dust. As she unlocked and opened the door to the driver's seat, she tilted her head to look up at him. "We might have conflicting opinions, Cade, but I can make a big difference here in Stokely. And I intend to do just that."

She climbed inside and reached for the armrest to pull the door closed. Before she did so, she gave him a smile so bright that it made his jaw ache. "Thanks again for all your help. I appreciate you being so neighborly."

He nodded once in acknowledgment, his tongue tied in knots.

As she started the ignition and pulled away, the tires of her truck bounced over the washboard road. Cade sat on his horse and stared after her, feeling withdrawn and out of sorts. He didn't agree with her assessment of the wild-horse situation, and yet he felt as though he'd just been scolded by his mother. In the nicest way possible.

He'd noticed the growing herds of horses becoming emaciated. But the beliefs planted in his mind throughout his childhood were hard to ignore. Wild horses should be left alone to live in freedom. The government shouldn't interfere. Right? Of course he was right!

Nope, he didn't like the new forest ranger, but he also couldn't deny that she seemed to know her business here. He just wished he didn't need to have any more dealings with her in the future. Since he was the wild-horse spokesman for the Toyakoi Shoshone Tribe, Cade figured that wasn't likely. He frequently participated in meetings and demonstrations to protect the wild horses.

Oh, yes. He'd see the new forest ranger again sometime soon. Much to his regret.

Chapter Two

❧

"How'd school go today?" Lyn tightened her fingers around the steering wheel as she pressed on the brake. Her car came to a halt at the only stoplight on Main Street in the town of Stokely. Population eleven thousand and twenty-three, including dogs, cats and gophers.

"None of the kids like me." Kristen's simple reply vibrated with hurt and anger.

"I'm sure that's not true, honey." Lyn glanced at her ten-year-old daughter, who sat next to her, tugging against her seat belt.

"Yes, it is."

"It just takes time to get to know everyone when you're the new kid in town. Maybe you could invite one of the girls in your class over to the house to play on Saturday." Lyn lightened her voice, trying to sound positive. Trying to encourage her daughter the only way she knew how.

The stoplight turned green and she pressed on the gas, moving slowly down the street.

"They'll never like me." Kristen tugged her skirt lower across the C-Leg prosthetic limb on her right leg as though trying to hide as much of the amputation as possible.

Lyn studied her child's tight profile and long white-blond hair. The girl was beautiful. If only the other children would treat her like a normal kid. But that was just the problem. Kristen wasn't normal. And she never would be. "How can they not like you? They hardly know you yet. We've only been here a couple of months."

Kristen tapped her knuckles hard against the socket of the prosthetic limb. "This is all they see, Mom. They call me peg leg and gimp."

Lyn's heart wrenched. Kids could be so cruel. If only they'd get to know Kristen, they'd learn what a smart, sweet girl she was. And so easy to love.

"I hate it here. I want to go home." Tears watered Kristen's voice as she flounced around and glared out the window.

"We are home, honey." Lyn wanted to cry, too, but didn't think that would do Kristen any good. Alone at night in her dark bedroom, Lyn allowed her emotions to flow across her pillow. But in the light of day, she must be strong. For both her and Kristen's sakes.

"Maybe you could wear blue jeans more often."

Dresses were easier in case Kristen needed to adjust her prosthetic limb, but pants hid the apparatus from view.

"It won't help. I limp and can't run. They know something's wrong with me. They don't like me."

Lyn's heart ached for her daughter. How she wished she could protect her from this pain. Even if they covered up the prosthesis, Kristen jerked so hard when she walked that people frequently stared at her. They knew immediately that the girl was impaired, but they didn't understand why. Lyn had even heard a woman in the grocery store yesterday whisper loudly that Kristen must be retarded. As if her leg had anything to do with her brain. In fact, the opposite was true. Kristen pulled top grades in science and math. If only she could walk better, she might fit in more.

"Well, I adore you," Lyn said with a smile.

"You don't count, Mom. You have to love me because I'm your kid."

Lyn snorted. "If that were true, there'd be a lot fewer abusive mothers in the world, honey. I love you more than my own life. And that's that."

Kristen tossed her head and huffed out a big sigh of exasperation. "You just don't understand."

Lyn understood more than Kristen realized. But friends and peer pressure were so important to a young girl. Especially a girl with only one leg. Moms didn't count at this point in life. If only it had been Lyn who had lost her leg in the accident. Not Kristen. Not her precious little girl.

Pressing on the brake again, Lyn came to a stop sign. A lance of vivid memory pierced her mind. The car crash had been caused by a drunk driver, now incarcerated in a state penitentiary. But that wouldn't restore Kristen's leg or bring Rob back. Nor did it ease Lyn's conscience over her part in what had happened. Though it'd only been a year earlier, Kristen had been so young. Only nine years old. They'd both lost the father and husband they dearly adored.

Rob. The love of Lyn's life.

She glanced in the rearview mirror. No one behind her, so she paused long enough to talk with Kristen for a few moments. Reaching across the seat, Lyn brushed her hand down the silken length of Kristen's hair. "I know this is hard, honey. But you're so pretty and smart. All your teachers tell me you're their best student. You've got a lot going for you. We've just got to keep trying."

Kristen shrugged off Lyn's hand, her voice thick with resentment. "You mean *I've* got to keep trying. I'm the one without a leg, not you. And Daddy's dead. The only reason I'm a good student is because I promised him."

Oh, that hurt. Not a day went by that she didn't feel guilty for surviving uninjured while her husband had died and her daughter lost her leg. But

Kristen was too young to understand how much a mother loved her child. Or just how much Lyn missed her husband.

"I know, honey. Please believe me—if I could take this pain from you, I would. I just want to help. We can't give up. Not ever."

Lyn might have reached over and hugged Kristen, but a driver pulled up behind them and blared the horn of their car. Lyn jerked her head around. Kathy Newton, a woman she'd recently met at Kristen's school, waved at them. Returning the gesture with a plastic smile, Lyn pressed on the gas. Two blocks later, she turned the corner and parked in front of the doctor's office before killing the motor.

"Maybe this new doctor can help you walk straighter," Lyn suggested. "Your old doctor highly recommended him."

A prosthesis specialist in such a small town was rare. Apparently this doctor was a former U.S. marine. Lyn had been told that he'd seen several of his buddies lose their limbs during the wars in Iraq and Afghanistan, and he'd done a lot of work in the field of prosthetics. And that could be really promising for Kristen.

"Nothing can help me walk without a limp. Everyone will always know something's wrong with me," Kristen said.

The ominous words were spoken to the glass windowpane. Kristen refused to look at her, and

Lyn couldn't blame her. Since the accident, Lyn could hardly stand to face herself. She'd hoped her transfer to this small ranching town might help make a difference for both of them. The slower pace. Fewer people. The jagged mountains and open, windswept valleys covered by bleached grass and sage. They both needed time to heal. Lyn had no outward scars, but inside, the accident had disfigured her beyond recognition. She'd never be the same again.

Neither would Kristen.

If only there was some way Lyn could go back in time, she'd find a reason to miss their appointment to view the Appaloosa mare. Their family had been so carefree that evening. Excited to buy Kristen's first horse. Both Lyn and Rob had been raised on a ranch, and Rob had been a regional rodeo champion during high school. They wanted to share their love of equines with their daughter. They'd discussed the idea for months. Kristen was fearless on a horse. She'd make such a great rider.

Lyn had just picked up Rob from work and was driving the car. Kristen had been sitting between them in the front seat, all of their seat belts securely fastened. They'd been talking. Laughing. And then Lyn turned onto a narrow street with a guardrail. The grille of a semitruck filled their view, followed by the sickening thunder of the crash. No time to react. No time to move.

Now Lyn closed her eyes tight, absorbing the memory as though it had just happened. If only she'd swerved and missed the oncoming truck. Maybe if she'd hit the brakes sooner. Or taken a different route. Anything to have changed the outcome.

Losing Rob had stolen all the joy in their lives. That night had been the last time they'd laughed together or felt genuinely happy.

The last time Lyn had prayed.

Filled with gloomy thoughts, she got out of the car and walked around to the passenger side to help Kristen. Again, the girl brushed aside Lyn's hands.

"I'll do it myself," the girl grumbled.

Lyn stood back, waiting nearby in case Kristen stumbled. An ocean of hurt separated them. Lyn wondered if they'd ever be close again.

Kristen hobbled toward the doctor's office. With each wrenching step, the foot of her cumbersome prosthesis smacked the cement sidewalk like a club. Lyn had to keep herself from flinching at the horrible sound. She followed close by, wishing Kristen would use her wheelchair more. But the girl refused. Lyn held her arms outstretched to catch Kristen in case she fell.

Inside the small office, Kristen plopped down onto a cushioned chair. An older man sat across from them, his denim shirt accented by a turquoise bolo tie. Twin streaks of gray marred his straight black hair. Parted in the middle, the long strands flowed past his shoulders, ornamented by a single white-and-gray feather. He held a beat-up cowboy hat in his leathery hands. Though he showed no expression on his tanned face, his intelligent black eyes gazed at them with unwavering frankness. The wide bridge of his nose and high cheekbones clarified his heritage. A proud American Indian. Probably Shoshone. Lyn knew they had a tribe here in Stokely.

Ignoring the man's piercing gaze, Lyn stepped over to the front counter and spoke to the receptionist. "I'm Lyn Warner. My daughter has an appointment at three-thirty."

"Yes, welcome. I'm Maya, and we've been expecting you." The matronly woman smiled, her rosy cheeks plumping. She swept a waterfall of straight black hair away from her face before handing Lyn a clipboard with papers attached. Maya also appeared to be of Shoshone heritage. "If you'll just fill out this information, I'll let the doctor know you're here."

Picking up a pen, Lyn sat beside Kristen and started writing. She was vaguely aware of Maya calling to the elderly man sitting across from them. He stood quietly and went to the counter to retrieve a bottle of pills.

"You take one of these every morning, Billie. And just so you know, I'm gonna call your wife to make sure you do. Helen will tell me if you're on your medication or not." Maya's voice sounded thick with warning.

Billie grunted a derogative reply. The pills rattled in the bottle as he shoved them into a pocket of his blue jeans. As he passed by to leave, he stared straight ahead, speaking not a single word. The epitome of dignity and cool disdain.

Lyn dug inside her purse for her insurance card. When she finished the paperwork, she returned the clipboard to Maya.

"Thanks. Why don't you come on back?" Maya indicated a side door.

Like always, Lyn stood beside Kristen as her daughter struggled to stand. Lyn's fingers itched to help Kristen, who was determined to do it by herself whether she looked odd and stumbled or not.

The girl braced her hands on the armrests, gained her balance, then clopped forward, her upper torso jerking back with each awkward step. Maya opened the door and stood there smiling until Kristen passed through, then led the way down a short hall to an examination room.

Inside, Kristen sat on the only chair, a grimace of pain showing her discomfort.

"Is it hurting you today?" Lyn asked.

"No." A short, curt word.

Lyn knew better. The wound had healed, but it'd only been a year. The stump continued to pain

Kristen whenever she wore her prosthesis. But the girl hated her wheelchair even more. And Lyn knew Kristen's autonomy would diminish with the chair.

Lyn was determined to speak with the doctor about this. The brave girl refused to show any more signs of weakness than what had been forced upon her. So daring and courageous. So determined not to quit in spite of the adversity she faced. If only this new doctor could help her somehow. If only—

The door rattled, and the doctor entered the room. Lyn's breath froze in her throat. The man glanced first at Kristen, then at the clipboard in his hand, but Lyn recognized him instantly. A tall, jet-eyed man with short, coal-black hair shaved high and tight like a U.S. marine. Like her, Lyn figured he was in his mid-thirties. With high, chiseled cheekbones, wide shoulders and long, solid legs. Dark and extremely handsome, in a dangerous sort of way. Except for his eyes. Fringed by thick lashes, they sparkled with gentle warmth.

"Cade!"

He looked up, his gaze mirroring her shock.

No, he couldn't be the angry rancher who thought Lyn was a threat to the mustangs. He didn't like her, he'd made that obvious last week when he'd saved her from the wild stallion. Surely he couldn't be Kristen's new doctor.

But he was. Oh, this day just kept getting worse.

* * *

Cade lifted his head, but didn't speak for several moments as he contemplated Lyndsy Warner's presence in his office. Her golden eyes held his like a vice grip, and he sensed her deep intelligence as she studied his face in return.

"You…you're Kristen's new doctor?" she asked.

"Apparently."

"Oh. I guess I didn't make the connection. But you said your name is Cade." Her expression looked deflated.

"That's right, although I'm Dr. Baldwin when I'm working in my office. I didn't expect to see you here, either."

Now he regretted not asking her full name when he'd met her in Secret Valley last week. He hadn't put it all together. Lyn was short for Lyndsy. He decided the name Lyn suited her better. Finding out the new forest ranger's daughter was one of his patients caught him completely off guard.

The tribal elders wouldn't like this. No, not at all.

His gaze took in the woman's skinny jeans, red blouse and white tennis shoes. Instead of a ponytail, she wore her long blond hair straight and soft around her face. But her eyes. A tawny-gold color, like cooked honey, sweet and smooth. Right now, she looked like a normal housewife, not a forest ranger. Not a threat to the wild horses. And certainly too young to have a daughter so old.

Likewise, she inspected him. The stethoscope hanging around his neck. The white smock he wore open over his blue chambray shirt. His denims and scuffed cowboy boots. He shifted nervously, wishing she'd stop looking at him.

"Um, when you rescued me from Buck, I didn't realize you were a doctor." A stiff smile curled her full lips, but didn't reach her beautiful eyes.

"Yeah, we didn't talk about that."

"I thought you were a rancher."

"I own Sunrise Ranch, but it's not big enough to grow crops and livestock anymore. My grandparents left the place to me. I just live there now."

"Oh." She continued to stare.

"You okay?" he asked, trying to hide his own feelings of confusion.

She looked away. "Yes, I'm sorry. It's just that you're not really what I imagined a prosthesis specialist would look like."

He made a soft scoffing sound, the heels of his boots thudding against the wooden floor. "Is that because I'm part Shoshone Indian?"

"No, not at all. I didn't know until now. Although that's fascinating, too."

She found his heritage fascinating? Ironically, that was how he would describe her. But he wasn't about to ask her to expand on her comment.

"I'm one-half Shoshone, on my mother's side.

Any less, and I wouldn't be eligible to belong to the tribe," he said.

With a Caucasian father and a Shoshone mother, he'd spent every childhood summer in Stokely with his mother's parents. He'd been in Afghanistan when his grandfather died and left him Sunrise Ranch. All his life, Cade had dreamed of becoming a doctor and opening a medical office here to benefit the Toyakoi Tribe, his Shoshone people. Now that he was here, he was haunted by memories of war. Only his faith in God kept him sane.

"Is my ethnicity a problem for you?" he asked.

She snorted. "Of course not. It's just that you seem so…so casual for a doctor."

Kaku, his grandmother, had always told him he was wild and untamed. Like the mustangs running free in Secret Valley. And yet, he wasn't wild. Not anymore. The war had changed him. He'd come to realize what was really important in life. God, family and living with honor. Now he just wanted to settle down and find peace. But one thing was missing. He had no family. They were all gone now. No one to share his hopes and dreams with. No one to love.

And he felt the emptiness like a hole in his heart.

"I'd look a bit out of place in Stokely if I ran around in a business suit." He reached for a stool on wheels. Pulling it over, he sat down in front of

Kristen. "And you didn't tell me your daughter was one of my new patients."

"I didn't realize at the time."

And whether he liked it or not, it appeared he'd now get to know them even better.

He faced Kristen, smiling to alleviate the girl's worried frown. "So, Kristen, how are you today?"

"Fine." Her voice sounded uncertain as she held her clasped hands tightly in her lap. Rather than happy and smiling, she looked anxious and withdrawn.

Frightened.

He made a pretense of scanning the clipboard. "You're what? Twelve, thirteen years old?"

Kristen's brow crinkled and she shook her head, looking away. Unsure of herself. Cade didn't like that. If he was going to help this child, he'd have to win her trust.

"I'm only ten, but I'll be eleven next November," she said.

Cade widened his eyes and drew back as though amazed. "Is that right? Well, you're sure pretty and you look older than your age. Very grown-up."

His flattery brought a flush of pleasure to the child's cheeks. Ah, he had her now. He loved helping people; he always had. But for some innate reason, he felt strongly that he must help this little girl feel better about herself. No matter who her mother was and what she did for a living.

"I've spoken to your doctor in Reno, and he's told me you're wearing a C-Leg prosthesis. Can I take a look?" Cade asked respectfully.

Kristen nodded, pulling her skirt up to a modest inch just above her skinny knees. Or rather, knee.

Setting the clipboard aside on the counter by the sink, Cade studied the mechanisms of the prosthesis. Pink and white scars crisscrossed the thighs of her amputated leg as well as her good leg. "Were both your legs injured?"

She nodded, but Lyn answered. "After the accident, they were only able to save her left leg."

Thank goodness they were able to save that much.

Cade reached for the socket of the prosthesis, his fingers pressing and pulling gently as he tested the fit around Kristen's stump.

"I don't think it fits properly," Lyn said. "She's had a recent growth spurt, which may have changed the fitting. It's hurting her. She isn't able to walk very well." She stepped near, hovering close by Kristen's side.

Cade liked the genuine concern he heard in Lyn's voice, and the tenderness as she brushed a protective hand over the girl's arm. It made her seem more human.

"We'll see." He bowed his head low, his attention on Kristen, but his words were for Lyn. "How'd you hear about my office?"

"Dr. Fletcher said you'd recently completed an internship with the Craig Stratich Group. I'm aware that they're leading specialists in prosthetics and research. I accepted my job in Stokely knowing there'd be a qualified doctor here to work with Kristen."

He grunted his acknowledgment, betraying his nervousness. The tribal leaders wouldn't want him treating the forest ranger's daughter, but he had very little choice. He certainly would never turn the girl away. Above all, he felt compassion for the child. She needed his help and he couldn't refuse.

He sat back and released a quick sigh. "You should know I'm not really a physical therapist. I'm not even a true prosthetist. I'm just a general practitioner who's worked a lot with prosthetics. Unfortunately, my office isn't currently set up to provide physical therapy for an amputee."

Lyn's brow crinkled, and her voice filled with apprehension. "Are you saying you can't treat Kristen?"

"No, I can work with your specialists in Reno. I'm sure we can come up with something to allow me to help you out, but I wanted you to know up front what I'm able to do." He made some mental notes of how he might install support bars for Kristen to hold on to as she learned to walk better. A floor mat and some practice stairs would help out, too. It wouldn't take much to create a therapy room for the little girl, yet it could make a big difference in the quality of her life.

"I understand," Lyn continued. "Dr. Fletcher said if anyone could help us, it was you."

Cade chuckled, unable to resist feeling pleased by the flattery. "I'll do my best. I wouldn't want to disappoint my old teacher."

"He also said you'd served several tours of duty as a marine in Afghanistan. When you got home, you finished medical school and focused on prosthetics because you had a good friend who lost his leg in the war."

Cade stiffened, taken off guard by how much she knew about him. She'd touched a raw nerve buried deep inside. Dallin had saved his life, putting himself in harm's way. Cade owed everything to Dal and much more. "Good ol' Dr. Fletcher. He always did have a wagging tongue."

"I didn't mean to be nosy," Lyn said. "It's just that Kristen's father was also a marine."

"I see. *Semper fi.*" Cade nodded in understanding. Just one more thing he didn't want to like about this woman.

"Always faithful," she said.

"I'm sure your husband was a good man." Cade almost groaned. Now he was making small talk with her.

"My daddy was the best," Kristen said.

Cade looked away, the knowledge of their loss

impacting him more than he liked. He patted Kristen on her good knee before rolling his stool backward. He didn't want to know about Lyn's dead husband. Or anything else about her, for that matter. "Why don't you stand and walk a few steps for me, sweetheart?"

The girl tossed a hesitant glance at her mother, then did as asked. Bracing her hands against the armrests of her chair, she lurched to her feet. She bit her bottom lip, obviously concentrating. Trying hard not to show her clumsiness. Lyn stood close by. Too close. Her hands were open and ready to catch the girl if she fell.

Kristen walked forward, bending slightly at the waist and sticking her bottom out before jerking the prosthetic leg forward. The end result was that she walked with a pronounced limp.

Cade stood and stepped over to give Kristen some guidance. He had to brush past Lyn, catching the tantalizing scent of some kind of fruity shampoo. Sweet and feminine. "Excuse me."

Lyn stepped back, but not far enough. Her gaze centered on Kristen like a mother eagle watching her young. And that's when Cade wondered if she was a bit overprotective.

"You definitely need a new prosthesis," Cade said. "We can get one fitted for you. I've got some good contacts for that. In the meantime, I'd like you to work on a few things for me. Can you do that?"

Kristen nodded, her blue eyes wide as she gazed up at him with a mixture of gratitude or doubt, he wasn't sure which.

"First, I don't think you're trusting your prosthesis enough. It won't collapse under you, so let it do the work for you. It's strong and can bear your weight. As you walk, you need to make sure your hip is over the foot."

He modeled the posture with his own hip and leg. "Set your weight down on the foot of your prosthesis before you take another step. Trust that it'll be there for you. Brace your hand on the wall if you need to support yourself. Then bring through your good leg. This will pull you up onto the toe of your prosthesis. Keep your hip over your foot. That will load the springs in the prosthetic foot so it'll help propel you forward on your next step."

Cade directed Kristen through the motions. When her hip and leg moved out of position, he gently pressed them back into proper order, and Kristen was soon taking less awkward steps.

Then he moved away. Without his aid, utter panic filled Kristen's eyes. "What if I fall?"

Lyn took a step toward her daughter, but Cade held out his hand to stop her from interfering. "Then you fall. What's the worst that'll happen?"

He waited, letting both daughter and mother digest this comment. Hoping Kristen realized that falling wasn't the worst thing she should fear.

"People will laugh," Kristen said.

"So let them. And what will you do?"

He hoped she didn't say she'd cry. He couldn't restore her leg, but he could help her toughen up so she could cope with her life.

"I get back up?" she asked.

A question, not a statement.

"Of course! Have you ever seen someone else fall down?" he asked.

The little girl nodded. Her mother looked tense and wary. Apprehensive.

"And did you laugh?" he asked.

"No." A vague response. She didn't understand what he was getting at. Not yet, anyway.

"Why not?"

"Because they fell down and might be hurt. I don't laugh because I know how it feels."

"Of course. But they don't just lie there. They get back up, right?"

Another nod.

He bent slightly at the waist so he could look her in the eyes. "Kids fall all the time, Kristen. You just gotta quit being afraid of it. I can teach you how to land on your bottom so it won't hurt as much. If you fall down, do you already know how to stand back up without help?"

She nodded, her eyes filled with a bit more trust, but not enough. Not yet. This poor girl had a lot of issues she needed to resolve if she was ever going to walk well and lead a normal, happy life.

"Then there's nothing to be afraid of, is there? You can get back up and walk on your merry way," he reiterated.

She looked down, her chin quivering. A strand of golden hair swept past her cheek. She looked so sweet and vulnerable.

Just like her mom.

"But kids laugh when I fall," she said.

His heart gave a powerful squeeze. "Then let them laugh. Show them it doesn't bother you one bit. And pretty soon, they won't laugh anymore."

Cade couldn't help wondering if Lyn had discussed this topic with Kristen. From the profound concern in her eyes, he knew the ranger cared deeply about her daughter. But maybe Kristen needed to hear this dialogue from someone besides her mom.

Maybe Lyn needed to hear it, too.

Taking a deep breath, Kristen took another step, and another. She pressed her tongue against her upper lip, seeming to concentrate on doing what he'd shown her. Learning to trust her prosthesis. Lyn tightened her hands into fists as though she fought the urge not to assist her child.

"Hey! I'm doing it better." Kristen smiled at her mom.

"You sure are, honey," Lyn agreed, her voice thick with emotion.

Cade's gaze darted to Lyn's face. Against his better judgment, he sympathized with the ranger and her cute daughter. How could he resist? He'd thought about telling Lyn he couldn't treat Kristen, but that went right out the window. Only an unfeeling ogre would turn their back on this woman and her child. They needed him. Maybe even more than Dal had needed him after he'd lost his leg.

"When you feel the resistance of the prosthetic toe, you tend to want to avoid it rather than learning to work with it. Believe in your prosthesis. Make it work for you. Trust it to be there," Cade advised.

"But it hurts." Kristen cringed.

"That's a different matter. You need a better-fitting socket. I can give you some extra thick socks to wear over your stump, but I think this socket is too loose. You have a bony prominence that needs a flexible area around it so it won't cause you pain."

"I knew something was wrong." Lyn sighed.

"We're gonna take care of that for you," Cade promised. "We'll get you fitted for a new prosthesis. I also want to give you some new exercises I think will strengthen your balance, abdomen and thighs."

He continued working with the child, learning her range of motion, strength and coordination. "You're quite limber and strong. I don't want you to lose that, so exercise every day. You just need more confidence."

A bit of hope filled Kristen's eyes. "Maybe when I get my new socket, I can play soccer with the other kids."

Lyn shook her head hard. "No, honey. You could get hurt doing that."

"Ahh," the girl groaned. "Dad would want me to try."

"Well, Dad isn't here." An unyielding edge of sternness laced Lyn's voice.

Definitely overprotective.

Cade stood silently, listening to this exchange. What had happened to Kristen's father? Why wasn't the guy here with his family?

"Kristen's father was killed in the accident when she lost her leg," Lyn explained as if she could read his thoughts.

From the sadness filling her eyes, Cade realized she'd divulged something very personal. Right now, she didn't look like the proficient forest ranger he'd met last week in Secret Valley. Now she just looked like a worried mom. Vulnerable and exposed. And that made him feel strangely protective of her.

No! He shook his head. The last thing he wanted was to feel sentimental toward this woman and her child. He was Kristen's doctor, nothing more. He must remain neutral. With all his patients.

Cade cleared his voice. "I'm sorry to hear that. But with a running prosthesis, I don't see why Kristen couldn't play soccer. Staying active will help her retain her range of motion."

He looked at Lyn, keeping his gaze insistent and unwavering.

Lyn's mouth tightened. "A running prosthesis won't be necessary. I doubt I can afford it anyway."

"We can talk about the cost later, but don't worry. We'll find a way to make it happen."

Why did he say that? Getting Kristen a running prosthesis at little or no cost would mean that he had to call in some huge favors. But if it meant she could run and play with the other children, he didn't mind going out of his way for this little girl.

Lyn tilted her head and gave him a stern look as she enunciated her next words. "No. I don't want Kristen hurt again."

Okay, he got it. In a way, Cade couldn't blame Lyn. Her husband had been killed and her daughter had lost her leg in a bad accident. No doubt Lyn didn't want to lose any more. He didn't argue the point, but their situation troubled him. Kristen's psychological needs were just as important as her physical needs. Being overprotective wasn't good if Kristen was to ever develop enough self-confidence and autonomy to lead a fairly independent life.

Cade would treat Kristen the best he could and

keep his distance from them otherwise. He and Lyn would never be friends. Nothing more than acquaintances. And for some odd reason, that made Cade feel strangely sad inside.

"I've heard of them, but what does Toyakoi stand for?" she asked.

"Mountain peak. We're a federally recognized Shoshone tribe with our own constitution."

"I see. And what can I do for you?"

"You said you go into the mountains on Fridays. I was wondering if it might be possible for me to accompany you now and then."

She hadn't expected this request. Not at all.

"I don't have time to go out every Friday."

He shrugged. "That's okay. I'd like to accompany you when you do have time."

"But what about your doctor's office? Don't you ve to work?" she asked.

"I only work in my office three days a week. e rest of the time I usually do research. For now, ike to spend some time with you, checking on mustangs."

e tilted her head, an edge of suspicion filling oice. "You mean you want to spy on me? To the big bad forest ranger is plotting the de- f all the wild-horse herds?"

esitated, his eyes crinkled with misgivings. lon't want to spy, but I do want you to show roblems so I can better understand how to wild horses."

nook her head and laughed, trying to he tense mood. "All right, I can accept

Chapter Three

"I like Dr. Baldwin." Kristen glanced at her mother as Lyn drove them home an hour later.

The girl rolled her car window down halfway, and the afternoon breeze teased golden wisps of hair that framed her oval face. A tangy smell hung in the air, and Lyn hoped it might rain up in the mountains. The wildlife sure needed the moisture.

"You do, huh?" Lyn kind of liked Cade, too, even if he didn't like her. The way he'd put Kristen at ease had impressed Lyn. It'd been a long time since she'd seen Kristen actually try to do what her doctor suggested. It wasn't that the girl was contrary, but rather, she seemed to have given up hope of ever walking normally again.

Truth be told, Lyn had almost given up, too.

"Yeah, he's a lot different from Dr. Fletcher."

Lyn silently agreed, but kept up the small talk, delighted to see her daughter smile again. "How so?"

"Dr. Fletcher is so…old."

Lyn laughed. "There's nothing wrong with old age as long as you get there, hon. Dr. Fletcher was always nice and helpful."

"Yeah, but Dr. Baldwin is handsome, and he smells nice. He's lots different," Kristen repeated.

Lyn laughed. Cade definitely smelled good. But he was unusual in other ways, too. His dark, gleaming eyes, his gentle frankness as he showed Kristen how to walk properly, his solid good looks. Lyn just hoped she could trust him to do what was best for her child.

"We've been too busy and gone way too long without you seeing a doctor," Lyn said. "Now that we're settled in, I'll get you to physical therapy every week."

"With Dr. Baldwin, that'll be nice," Kristen said.

Hmm. Maybe Kristen had a small crush on the attractive doctor.

As they ate dinner that evening, then prepared for bed, Kristen talked nonstop about Cade. Today had been a great start, and Lyn felt an inkling of optimism for the first time since Rob's death. Perhaps Cade was just what Kristen needed.

The last thing Lyn expected the following morning was Cade showing up unannounced at her ranger's office. Looking up from a pile of paperwork stacked on her desk, she found his tall silhou-

ette outlined in the doorway and inhaled a sharp breath. He'd appeared silently out of nowhere, and she wondered how long he'd been watching her work.

"Cade! You startled me." She glanced behind him, speculating on where Cindy, her office manager, was and how he'd gotten past her without interception.

He gave a lazy shrug. "Sorry. I had an ide and decided to stop by to see if you might be ar nable."

He didn't smile, but his gentle eyes betraye inner feelings. He wanted something. From

"You got a minute?" he asked, his thumb ha ing casually through the belt loops of his b

She stood and indicated a chair across desk. "Sure! Please, sit down."

He sat, lifting one long leg to cross the ankle over his opposite knee. She cau Sh aroma of spice and leather, and her her v to the hollow of his throat where a t see if ran along the front of his throat. A mise he'd been sliced by a knife. He h

She swallowed and focused "No, I what did you want to talk abou me the

"I'm actually here in an of help the began. "I'm the wild-horse She s Toyakoi Tribe." He paused lighten t information sink in.

Chapter Three

"I like Dr. Baldwin." Kristen glanced at her mother as Lyn drove them home an hour later.

The girl rolled her car window down halfway, and the afternoon breeze teased golden wisps of hair that framed her oval face. A tangy smell hung in the air, and Lyn hoped it might rain up in the mountains. The wildlife sure needed the moisture.

"You do, huh?" Lyn kind of liked Cade, too, even if he didn't like her. The way he'd put Kristen at ease had impressed Lyn. It'd been a long time since she'd seen Kristen actually try to do what her doctor suggested. It wasn't that the girl was contrary, but rather, she seemed to have given up hope of ever walking normally again.

Truth be told, Lyn had almost given up, too.

"Yeah, he's a lot different from Dr. Fletcher."

Lyn silently agreed, but kept up the small talk, delighted to see her daughter smile again. "How so?"

"Dr. Fletcher is so…old."

Lyn laughed. "There's nothing wrong with old age as long as you get there, hon. Dr. Fletcher was always nice and helpful."

"Yeah, but Dr. Baldwin is handsome, and he smells nice. He's lots different," Kristen repeated.

Lyn laughed. Cade definitely smelled good. But he was unusual in other ways, too. His dark, gleaming eyes, his gentle frankness as he showed Kristen how to walk properly, his solid good looks. Lyn just hoped she could trust him to do what was best for her child.

"We've been too busy and gone way too long without you seeing a doctor," Lyn said. "Now that we're settled in, I'll get you to physical therapy every week."

"With Dr. Baldwin, that'll be nice," Kristen said.

Hmm. Maybe Kristen had a small crush on the attractive doctor.

As they ate dinner that evening, then prepared for bed, Kristen talked nonstop about Cade. Today had been a great start, and Lyn felt an inkling of optimism for the first time since Rob's death. Perhaps Cade was just what Kristen needed.

The last thing Lyn expected the following morning was Cade showing up unannounced at her ranger's office. Looking up from a pile of paperwork stacked on her desk, she found his tall silhouette outlined in the doorway and inhaled a sharp breath. He'd appeared silently out of nowhere, and she wondered how long he'd been watching her work.

"Cade! You startled me." She glanced behind him, speculating on where Cindy, her office manager, was and how he'd gotten past her without interception.

He gave a lazy shrug. "Sorry. I had an idea and decided to stop by to see if you might be amenable."

He didn't smile, but his gentle eyes betrayed his inner feelings. He wanted something. From her.

"You got a minute?" he asked, his thumbs hanging casually through the belt loops of his blue jeans.

She stood and indicated a chair across from her desk. "Sure! Please, sit down."

He sat, lifting one long leg to cross the booted ankle over his opposite knee. She caught his subtle aroma of spice and leather, and her gaze lowered to the hollow of his throat where a thin, white scar ran along the front of his throat. Almost as though he'd been sliced by a knife.

She swallowed and focused on his face. "So, what did you want to talk about?"

"I'm actually here in an official capacity," he began. "I'm the wild-horse representative for the Toyakoi Tribe." He paused as though letting this information sink in.

"I've heard of them, but what does Toyakoi stand for?" she asked.

"Mountain peak. We're a federally recognized Shoshone tribe with our own constitution."

"I see. And what can I do for you?"

"You said you go into the mountains on Fridays. I was wondering if it might be possible for me to accompany you now and then."

She hadn't expected this request. Not at all.

"I don't have time to go out every Friday."

He shrugged. "That's okay. I'd like to accompany you when you do have time."

"But what about your doctor's office? Don't you have to work?" she asked.

"I only work in my office three days a week. The rest of the time I usually do research. For now, I'd like to spend some time with you, checking on the mustangs."

She tilted her head, an edge of suspicion filling her voice. "You mean you want to spy on me? To see if the big bad forest ranger is plotting the demise of all the wild-horse herds?"

He hesitated, his eyes crinkled with misgivings. "No, I don't want to spy, but I do want you to show me the problems so I can better understand how to help the wild horses."

She shook her head and laughed, trying to lighten the tense mood. "All right, I can accept that. But remember, I want to help the mustangs, too, Cade. I really do."

"I hope that's true. I've been thinking over what you said last week about the wild horses, wildlife and domestic livestock all being equally important. I think we should work together to find some satisfactory resolutions."

"But last week you weren't interested in hearing my ideas."

He gave a lazy shrug. "I've reconsidered."

Hmm. Maybe this could be a good thing. Working together with the Toyakoi Tribe might help alleviate a lot of tension between the horse advocates and the government entities.

"You realize the Bureau of Land Management has jurisdiction over the wild horses, not the Forest Service. I can't decide anything for the mustangs," she said.

"Yes, but I also know you have the power to call the BLM in to look at the situation and then get them to consider rounding up the mustangs and move some of them off your ranger district."

He made a valid point.

"It's not *my* ranger district, Cade. I'm merely the overseer here. And I won't pretend I'm not very close to being forced to call in the BLM now. The horse and burro population grows by about twenty percent each year. Without any natural predators, that means they double in size about every four years. There's just too many of them, and the damage has become quite serious."

She didn't mention the myriad of ranchers she had breathing down her neck, asking her to do something about the problem soon. She'd handle the ranchers the same way she would the Shoshone Tribe. With honesty, professionalism and tact.

He sat back in his cracked leather chair. "Look, Mrs. Warner. All I'm asking is that you involve me in your decisions. I can do a lot to talk about this with the Shoshone people and keep this problem from blowing up into a big hornets' nest. We might be able to assist with some decisions, if you'll let us."

Yes, she was highly aware of that. Maybe a partnership of sorts would be wise. If Cade saw firsthand what she was dealing with in the mountains and valleys, he could take that information back to the wild-horse advocates and gain some support for what must be done.

"Okay, you're welcome to come along—on one condition," she said.

"And what's that?"

"You call me Lyn. I don't like formality if I can avoid it. I'd like us to be friends."

He blinked, his eyes glinting with hesitancy. "Okay, I'll call you Lyn. When is your next trip? What are the plans?"

She noticed his omission of them becoming

friends. That was okay. She'd learned long ago that she could work with people she had no fondness for. As long as she maintained her composure and worked professionally, it wouldn't be a problem. At least not for her.

"I'll be taking a horse trailer up into the McClellan Mountains on Friday and then riding into Barton's Canyon to look at the creek there. If you want to tag along, you'll need to bring your own horse. We can ride together, but plan to stay out all day."

He flashed her a devastating smile. "Deal. I'll even pack us a lunch."

"That's not necessary. I can bring my own food."

"I want to do it. I promise you won't regret it."

She let the subject drop. What she ate for lunch was the least of her concerns.

They made a few more arrangements, with Lyn planning to drive out to Sunrise Ranch so they could load his horse into her Forest Service trailer. Then they'd drive up onto the mountain and unload the horses. They'd spend the entire day riding across some very rugged terrain together.

Lyn doubted her sanity for agreeing to Cade's proposal. Being near this man made her jittery for some peculiar reason. She tried to tell herself that working with him would help with resolving the wild-horse problems. But it could backfire on her, too. If he didn't like what he saw or didn't believe what she told him, he could make a lot of trouble for her with the Toyakoi Tribe. Then she'd be forced to override him and call in the BLM anyway.

The last ranger on this district had dealt with a lot of angry people and even a death threat. Lyn wanted to avoid that, if possible. If she disagreed with Cade, what impact might that have on Kristen? Cade Baldwin was now Kristen's doctor. Lyn certainly didn't want him for an enemy. No, not one bit.

This was a mistake. Cade never should have come here to Lyn Warner's office and asked to be included in her visits to the wild horses. No matter what she thought, he didn't want to make trouble. But neither did he want to see the mustangs driven to and fro by a helicopter, captured in a corral, and then loaded on a truck to be transported miles and miles away from their home.

"What exactly are you planning to look at on Friday?" he asked, trying to ignore a large picture on her wall of a black stallion with a long flowing tail and mane as he raced across a meadow of green grass. Absolutely spectacular. Remembering Lyn's camera, Cade wondered if she'd taken the picture.

Her chair squeaked as she sat forward. "Being new to this ranger district, I've never viewed Barton's Canyon. I've been told that the creek is in bad shape, and I want to see it for myself. The Forest Service has worked hard to build up a nice band of desert bighorn sheep in that area, and I want to make sure we don't lose any of them."

Cade thought the bighorns could surely cause as much damage as the horses. "How many sheep are we talking about?"

"Approximately thirty-three, including rams."

Okay, maybe not. Even Cade knew there were many more mustangs running wild across the range than there were sheep. He'd seen the horses himself and knew the bighorn were way outnumbered.

"You like bighorn sheep, don't you?" she asked.

Her question took him off guard. "Of course. I love all the wildlife."

"Good. Because I'm told they're in danger right now. Not enough food and difficulty getting to a decent water source."

But how could the mustangs cause that problem? The horses were just living out there, trying to survive. It couldn't be so cut-and-dried. There must be another reason the bighorn sheep were in danger. Maybe this was just another scare tactic. A strategy Cade had seen other government employees use in the past. Next he expected Lyn to blame the mustangs for the demise of the mule deer and antelope, too.

Something inside him hardened. "I hope you're not going to blame all of this on the wild horses."

She took a deep inhale and paused for several moments as though choosing her words carefully.

"I'll tell you what, Cade. Let's ride up Barton's Canyon and take a look. I'd like to view it before I make any judgment calls. Maybe my people are wrong in their reports and there isn't a problem. That would make my job much easier. I wouldn't have to disturb the horses. But if something is wrong, it'll speak loud and clear, and then I'll need to deal with it accordingly."

Her reasoning impressed him. No thumping her fist on the desk. No insisting the horses were to blame. If she could stay impartial until she saw something wrong, then he could, too. Or at least, he hoped he could. "That sounds fair to me. But what kinds of problems have your people reported?"

Her brow furrowed. "Let's just wait. If something's wrong, we'll see it. Let's educate ourselves first, and then we can talk about it in depth, okay?"

Again, her insight startled him. He hadn't expected the new forest ranger to be so reasonable. And that made him even more suspicious that she might have hidden motives.

"Okay." He answered slowly, afraid he might have to defer to her judgment on this topic. After all, what did he really know about vegetation and wild animals? As a medical doctor, he'd studied plenty of science and biology. He was definitely smart enough to see through a shell game. But he knew almost nothing about ecosystems, watersheds, wildlife and grazing needs.

What if there was something wrong? And what if Lyn blamed the problems on the wild horses? Cade could write his senators on behalf of the Shoshone Tribe, but the BLM had the law on their side. They'd do whatever they deemed was right.

"And if we don't find anything wrong, will you leave the mustangs alone?" He didn't want the bighorn sheep and other wildlife to suffer, but neither did he want her to move the horses if they were innocent.

"Absolutely."

But in her eyes, he saw doubt. And a bit of regret. And that gave him a shivery foreboding. "You seem skeptical."

"I am," she admitted. "I have a master's degree in ecology, and I do this job for a living, Cade. I've seen this situation before. The problems aren't always easy to address, but the cause seems to be consistent in these circumstances."

In other words, she was almost certain she'd find problems, which would require her to act against the horses.

"Are you sure you can be objective toward the mustangs?" he asked, feeling a bit cynical.

She nodded, her eyes narrowing. "Oh, yes. Remember I'm here to protect *all* the wild animals, including the mustangs. I don't have the luxury of preferring one animal over another. I'm a conservationist, not a preservationist. All of these animals are important to the area."

Cade wanted to believe her. He really did. But there'd been trouble in the past, and he'd grown accustomed to distrusting government employees. But not at the expense of the desert bighorn sheep. And the mule deer. And many other species he couldn't name right now.

No doubt Lyn could name them all.

"Okay, I can accept that." As he said the words, he hoped he meant them. For now, he'd wait until Friday and see what happened from there. He'd know soon enough if the horses were the problem. And then he'd do everything in his power to help save them.

As he left Lyn's office, he couldn't help feeling a bit on edge. As if he'd been told he had a large lump in his throat that needed a biopsy to determine if it was malignant or benign. The unknown made him nervous.

He was absolutely certain of one thing. If Lyn Warner had ulterior motives, he'd ferret them out. Just as she must trust him to provide the best medical care for her daughter, Cade must also trust Lyn to do what was right for the wild horses.

And there lay the crux of the problem. Neither of them fully trusted each other. At least, not yet.

Chapter Four

Friday morning, Lyn watched as Cade Baldwin stepped out onto the front porch of his white frame house. She tried to smile as she parked her green Forest Service truck and horse trailer at the side of his wide, graveled driveway.

He stood waiting as she got out of the truck. Dressed in cowboy boots and tight blue jeans, he wore a gray chambray shirt that embraced his muscled arms and the width of his shoulders like a fitted sheet of fine linen. Even from this distance, she caught the flash of his white teeth as he squinted against the morning sun. He tugged a battered hat low across his forehead, shadowing his eyes. He stared back, taking in her ranger uniform, a deep frown creasing the corners of his full lips.

With a couple flips of her hands, she pulled her long, blond hair back into a ponytail and walked toward him. A blue-coated Australian cow dog stood beside Cade, panting and wagging his tail happily. Lyn wasn't surprised when the dog didn't rush her. Real cow dogs were highly trained, calm and obedient. This one seemed especially well behaved.

"Good morning, Cade," Lyn called.

"Morning." A monotone reply. No lilt in his voice.

The greeting seemed to signal the dog. He ran to meet her, snuffling at her legs. She bent down and held out a hand, palm up, waiting for the animal to sniff her skin before she petted and scratched his ears.

"Hi, fella. You got a name?"

"Gus," Cade supplied in a rather brusque tone.

She glanced at Cade's forearms and hands where a myriad of white scars blemished his golden skin. Like he'd been sliced repeatedly with a knife. Noticing her gaze, he quickly rolled his sleeves down, hiding his arms from view.

She stepped back from the dog, trying to be as pleasant as possible. After all, Cade was the one who'd asked to join her, not the other way around. "You ready to go?"

"Yeah, Flash is over here." He walked toward the corral, moving with the slow grace of a man who knew his place in the world and wasn't afraid to do what had to be done.

A bay gelding stood with his head over the rail

fence, ears pricked forward with interest. A handsome mustang.

While Cade carried his saddle to put inside the back of Lyn's horse trailer, she glanced around his yard. Yellow tulips bloomed along the side of the two-story house, and there wasn't a weed in sight. Tall, straight fences showed good repair, the house wearing a fresh coat of paint. She could find no fault with its upkeep.

"You have a beautiful place here. A very large house," Lyn remarked.

"Thank you."

She glanced at the white wraparound porch and chained swing that swayed gently in the breeze. For just a moment, she imagined herself sitting there in the evening with a glass of lemonade in her hand. She envisioned Kristen running across the green lawn and laughing. No limp. No holes in their hearts. A happy family once more.

Lyn studied the upper floor where three wide windows and shutters trimmed with blue paint gazed down at her. A cheery place she longed to explore. "How many bedrooms do you have?"

Cade opened the corral gate and led Flash toward the horse trailer. "Three downstairs and five up. There's also three baths, a large kitchen, mudroom and living room with a rock fireplace. The guesthouse out back has three more bedrooms and another full bath. Are you in the market?"

She blinked. "No, I was just curious."

"Good, because I'd never sell this place. I just finished renovating the downstairs bathroom, complete with a walk-in shower and jetted tub. The work is good therapy."

"Therapy for what?"

He frowned as though he'd confided too much. "I just like to stay busy."

Hmm. She could read a lot in what he didn't say. Rob had fought in the Gulf War. He'd liked to stay busy, too. It helped him forget a lot of trauma, and Lyn wondered if it was the same for Cade. Though she'd never been to war, she understood the feeling. "What's the guesthouse for?"

"Years ago, it used to be a bunkhouse filled with wranglers who helped work the ranch. Now it just sits empty."

"And you live here all alone?"

"Yep."

She hurried to open the door and lower the ramp to the trailer. "Where's your family?"

He hesitated, a hint of sadness in his expressive voice. "I have a cousin living back east, but the rest are all gone now. My grandfather died last spring and willed me what's left of the ranch. Over the years, he'd sold off pieces of it here and there."

No wonder Cade would never sell. The ranch must have a lot of sentimental value for him. "I'm sorry to hear of your loss."

Her Appaloosa mare stood inside the trailer, and Flash neighed a low greeting and waved his head. The other horse nickered in return, and Flash walked right up the ramp without any urging. Cade closed the metal door behind him.

Lyn glanced at Gus, who hadn't left her side. "Your dog seems pretty calm. Would he like to go with us?"

Cade nodded. "That's thoughtful of you. He takes my commands and does well up on the mountain. He won't chase any wildlife, unless I ask him to."

That was good enough for Lyn. Without a word, she opened the door and gave a shrill whistle. "Come, Gus!"

The dog's ears pricked forward, and he stared at the woman for several moments as though assessing her. She wasn't his master, after all, but she'd worked with cow dogs when she'd been a kid on her parents' ranch. The dog decided she was okay and raced to the door, hopping up inside.

Pulling his cowboy hat off his head, Cade wiped his brow. "Looks like he minds you better than he does me."

Lyn chuckled as she got into the driver's seat and started the engine. She waited for Cade to join her and snap on his seat belt. With Gus sitting between them, panting, Lyn put the truck in gear and pulled out of the yard.

They didn't speak as she took the dirt road leading up to the McClellan Mountains. The desert rolled out before them, beautiful with its austere sage and golden-brown hues. She pointed at a rocky outcropping bedecked by blue lupine and mountain sunflowers. "Isn't that pretty? Spring is finally here."

Cade blinked in confusion, then nodded. "I've been up this road zillions of times, but never noticed any flowers before."

She kept her gaze in front of her, navigating the twisty turns with ease. "I suppose war and medical school are a big distraction. It's hard to stop our busy lives long enough to notice the beautiful world we live in."

He didn't comment. As they climbed in elevation, the vegetation became more scrubby. A trail of PJ's hugged the dirt road leading into the canyon. Silver-colored rocks and gravel littered the vast hills with clear views of the mountains flowing beyond the horizon. Desolate or not, Lyn loved this place already. When she went up into the mountains like this, she could almost forget her troubles for a short time.

"Isn't the desert beautiful?" she asked, not necessarily looking for an answer.

"I think so," he said, then clamped his mouth shut as though he regretted speaking.

At the mouth of Barton's Canyon, Lyn pulled the

truck over to a flat area and killed the motor. "We'll ride the rest of the way from here on horseback."

"Whatever you say."

They unloaded their horses. A quiet camaraderie settled between them as they worked. Without her asking, the doctor lifted her blanket and saddle onto the back of her horse. Lyn could easily do the chore, but Cade's thoughtfulness impressed her and she thanked him. Gus lazed patiently beneath the wide spread of a cottonwood, not at all bothered by the waiting.

"This is Applejack." Lyn patted the neck of her white Appaloosa mare.

"Is that a Forest Service horse or your own?" Cade eyed the government brand on the horse's rump.

"Forest Service. I don't own a horse anymore, although Kristen keeps begging me to buy her one." Lyn drew in a deep breath and let it go. "Most kids want a puppy, but not my Kristen. She wants a horse—as if she could ever ride."

"Why can't she ride?"

She waited for Apple to exhale before tightening the cinch on her saddle. "I think you know the answer to that. Kristen can barely walk, let alone ride horses. I think she wants one because her dad loved them so much. She wants to play soccer and girls' basketball, too."

He pulled the reins up over the gelding's head

and stepped up onto his horse. "So let her. There's no reason she can't do all those activities."

Everything within Lyn rebelled, and she looked at him as if he'd gone daft. "No, I don't want her falling off a horse or getting knocked down by an angry teammate. She doesn't move very fast, and she's been hurt enough."

They both had. If only they could start to heal now. But it seemed an impossible goal, always out of reach. Everything was so difficult. The hospital and doctor visits, the continuous pile of medical bills, shuttling Kristen back and forth from school, the girl's constant sullen attitude. Everything had become an exhausting task. And if losing Rob wasn't bad enough, it now seemed there was a wide gulf of anger between mother and daughter. And Lyn didn't know how to breach the void.

"Don't you think Kristen should decide what's too difficult for her to do?" Cade asked. "Maybe she figures getting hurt is worth it to try and succeed at new things. Kids need to try different activities to help build their confidence."

Lyn's mouth hardened. This man didn't know her or her daughter. Not really. One doctor's visit didn't give him the right to tell her how to raise her own child. "I'm her mother. I know what's best for her."

She ignored his deep frown and turned her back on him as she adjusted the halter over Apple's muzzle. As she climbed into the saddle, she hoped Cade would let the subject drop.

"What if I help Kristen?" he persisted. "I'm pretty good with horses and could give her riding lessons. It'd strengthen her legs and back, which would help her walk better, too. As her doctor, I highly recommend she try anything she likes. Let her live her life, Lyn."

Hearing him say her first name caused her face to heat up like road flares. A feeling of panic made her arms tremble, and she shook her head. "I…I can't take that chance. Kristen's a smart kid. She'll go to college one day and get a good job. There are lots of things she can do to support herself with her feet safely on the ground. She doesn't need to ride horses in order to live a fulfilled life."

"I agree, but she has to learn what makes her happy. We all do. You can't force her to be what she's not any more than you can inhibit what she likes doing. Riding might give her a lot more self-confidence with walking."

"So will good grades."

Cade didn't respond, thank goodness. She didn't want to get into an argument with this man over the right way to raise her child. She'd love for Kristen to be able to run, jump, play and do anything she liked. But she couldn't. Lyn didn't want her daughter to suffer any more heartbreak. And so the answer must be no.

As they rode through the sage-covered canyon, Lyn tried to push aside the horrible memories swamping her mind. Recollections of the sickening crash and its aftermath in the emergency room. And then the anguish at the cemetery as they bid farewell to a key member of their family. Kristen hadn't been there, still in the hospital and too sick to attend her own father's funeral. Cade's suggestion that Lyn let Kristen ride horses rubbed hard against the fears she'd hidden deep inside. The doctor didn't know all that she'd lost. He didn't understand.

No, Lyn couldn't afford to take any more chances. Not with her only child.

Cade couldn't stop thinking of ways to help Lyn realize she was being too protective. It must be so hard for Kristen, wanting to ride and play when her mother wouldn't even let her try. Cade was Kristen's doctor, but he had no right to make decisions for Lyn's little girl. He just wished he could help them somehow.

Determined to focus on the work at hand, he called for Gus to stay nearby as he pulled Flash up and looked down on a scraggly meadow filled with bleached cheatgrass. His heart plummeted at what he saw. As a kid, he remembered the area being filled with lush, green vegetation. Now the area seemed like a vast wasteland.

From this high vantage point, he had a great view of the entire valley. At least five bands of horses roamed the vicinity. Cade mentally counted forty-three in all.

Spring foals with spindly legs frolicked across the dry, dead earth. A mare rolled, grunting with enjoyment as she covered herself from head to tail in dust. The stallion of each band kept a watchful eye on the other herds in case they got too close. Mares snuffled at the barren ground in a futile search for something to eat. Others stood knee-deep in the muddy stream, drinking at leisure.

Reaching into her saddlebag, Lyn pulled out a pair of binoculars. Lifting them to her eyes, she focused on Buck and his herd.

"Something wrong?" Cade asked.

"Yes." She lowered the binoculars and shook her head. "One of Buck's mares is missing. The one with the little black foal and the white tail and mane."

Cade remembered them well. The filly was young, about three months old and pretty as can be. A unique pinto, almost completely black. "I'm sure they'll turn up."

"I hope so. A lot can happen out here. Mountain lions love to target young foals. But even if the filly was killed, the mare should still be here."

"I'm sure they're fine, resting in the shade of a

tree someplace. The broomtails are beautiful, don't you think?"

Broomtails. A slang word he used for wild mustangs.

"Yes, but still shedding their winter coats," Lyn agreed.

A deep warmth filled Cade's chest as he watched the wild horses he loved. The low rumbling sound of a sage grouse rose above the air. Cade saw the bird, a male. Its long, pointed tail feathers fanned out as its white chest bubbled out in a display meant to win him a mate. At least this part of Cade's life hadn't changed. But he couldn't help wondering what had killed the lush meadows of grass. And why weren't there more sage grouse? There used to be dozens of the interesting birds living here.

"They're all hungry." Lyn's eyes glowed, but her forehead creased with worry.

And Cade knew why. Without being told, he could see for himself that there wasn't enough feed in this valley for so many wild horses. Lyn's concern shook Cade's preconceived notions about rangers. He'd never expected her to fret over the mustangs the way he did. Lyn was an enigma, and he didn't know quite what to make of her.

"Look how lean they all are," she said.

He frowned, taking in the horses' shaggy condition and boney rib cages. "They're coming out of winter, but they should be okay now that the grass is growing again."

Lyn shook her head. "No grass is growing here. There's water, but nothing to eat. This meadow should be filled with needle and thread grass and three-awns."

Cade knew the names of the vegetation well. "The horses must be eating something."

He pointed at a herd grazing along the stream. From this distance the mustangs didn't seem agitated, but they lifted their heads, ears pricked forward as they peered at the human intruders. Gus stood at attention, but he didn't move. And he wouldn't, not unless Cade gave him a command.

"They're here for the water, not food," Lyn observed.

"They'll find grass elsewhere." They always did. But even Cade knew they wouldn't eat the dried cheatgrass and patches of mule's ear blotting the landscape below.

"Not in this meadow, nor the hills surrounding us," she said. "These horses need Great Basin wild rye and western wheatgrass. With all this cheatgrass, we'll be fighting wildfire up here by July. There won't be any palatable feed late in the year for wild animals to bring their young up to eat. Adult animals need healthy grass in order to produce milk for their young. And there won't be any."

"They'll find it on the other side of the mountain," Cade insisted, trying to be positive. Trying to ignore the sinking feeling that settled in his stomach.

Lyn tilted her head back for several moments as if accepting the inevitable. Then she looked at him, her gold eyes drilling into his. "There's no water over there, Cade. It's a long journey back and forth. They'll burn off any calories they take in. That'll be awfully hard on their young."

He stared at her, unable to answer. For centuries, the mustangs had roamed these lands, brought here by the Spaniards. They'd always been here. Of course, he couldn't remember their herds being so numerous in the past. He couldn't remember ever seeing so many wild horses before.

"These horses will starve to death, beginning with the young foals." A raw sadness filled Lyn's voice.

Cade didn't like her prediction. His expression must have told her so.

"Sorry, but I can't sugarcoat it, Cade. We have to do something. Wildlife populations like deer and antelope are controlled through hunting and natural predators. Cows are controlled by the limits outlined in the grazing permits we issue to ranchers. But horses were introduced here by mankind. We don't hunt them, and they have few natural enemies. Federal law prohibits people from capturing or harassing them. So their herds keep growing.

Starvation will thin out the herds, but it's a cruel way to die. I don't want to ignore the situation and lose our desert bighorn sheep and other wildlife, too."

He agreed, but surely something could be done to help these horses survive without moving them.

"Look at that!" He pointed toward an isolated place upstream where three bighorn sheep stood waiting.

Lyn gazed at the animals for several moments. "They want water, but they can't drink here."

Cade didn't understand. Of course they could drink. The creek was here for the taking. "Why do you say that?"

She nodded toward the bands of horses languishing around the creek beds. "Most wild animals come in and drink, then leave. But not horses. They mill around and stay forever. It's in their nature. But it damages the creek and keeps other smaller animals like deer and elk from being able to drink. In the process of waiting, the bighorn sheep lose precious feeding time."

She nudged her horse forward down the gentle incline and he followed, taking her lead. Gus padded after them, his paws raising puffs of dust into the air.

As they reached the bottom of the hill, one band of mustangs began to amble away from the stream, not liking the nearness of the man and woman.

The bighorn sheep followed right behind the wild horses, finally able to dip their heads toward the water for a long drink.

Lyn pulled up her Appaloosa, sitting quietly and watching. "The bighorn must be desperate for water to stay and drink even with us so nearby. The only reason they're surviving here is because the stream is long enough that they can find places to slip into that aren't monopolized by the horses."

Cade's mouth tightened as he thought this over. He'd promised to be open-minded, but he hadn't expected her to point these things out with such clarity. Seeing how the bands of mustangs hoarded the creek surprised him. The meadow seemed so desolate now.

Dead.

"Notice there are very few sage grouse here also. They're endangered now," she said.

"Because of the mustangs?" Impossible.

She nodded. "The horses wipe out the vegetation along the streams. The sage grouse eat seeds, young sprouts and insects along the waterways. No vegetation means no bugs and nothing for the sage grouse to eat. The little birds just can't compete with the big horses."

He didn't like this explanation, but couldn't help remembering a time when his grandfather brought him here to this exact meadow to hunt sage grouse. Now the bird was in danger of extinction. That made his heart ache. "I never really thought about the impact larger animals have on vegetation and that it filters down to the food source for birds."

She nodded. "And fish. It really requires balance within the entire watershed. And right now, this ecosystem is seriously out of balance."

The afternoon sun beat down on them, and Cade wiped a bead of moisture from his brow. Lyn dismounted and he joined her, reaching into his saddlebags for their lunch. For almost an hour, they sat against the hill and surveyed the happenings below. They spoke in muted tones as they ate the thick roast-beef sandwiches and fresh fruit he'd prepared. Lyn tossed pieces of meat to Gus, and Cade popped the lid on a bottle of water and poured it into a bowl for the dog.

"Thanks for lunch. This is delicious," Lyn said with a smile.

A smidgeon of mayonnaise blotted the corner of her mouth. Cade reached up and wiped it away with his finger. Touching her soft skin sent a current of electricity through him as she drew back in surprise. Looking away, he ignored the flush of embarrassment heating his face. He felt too comfortable around this woman. She was too easy to talk to. He mustn't forget who she was, or his resolve to save the mustangs.

"Thanks." She gave a low laugh and wiped her mouth with a kerchief.

"Have you named all these stallions?" He nodded toward the horses, reminding himself this outing was all about business.

"Yes, and some of the bachelor stallions, too."

"What do you call that stud over there?" He pointed at a piebald with a black mane. Very pretty.

"Ira."

"That's an odd name for a horse," he said.

"Yeah, it comes from the Bible and means watchful. Notice he's always standing at attention? He's the watchdog of the group. He drinks last, after his mares and foals have had their fill. A very attentive father."

Cade grunted. He hadn't expected this woman to be so observant of the horses' traits, or versed in the Bible, either. His entire family had demonized forest rangers. He'd never considered that they might love the Lord like he did. "You read the Bible often?"

She shook her head and scowled. "Not lately."

He didn't push the subject. It wasn't his business. But he sensed something in her tone. A twinge of bitterness he figured must have something to do with losing her husband. Instead, he jutted his chin toward a honey-colored palomino. "And that one?"

"Beeswax. He's always agitated and in everyone else's business. Notice how he never stands still? And see that ugly scar on his rump? It's old, but

I'll bet he had a run-in with a mountain lion when he was a colt."

Cade fully agreed with her assessment.

"And what about that one over there?" He pointed at a powerfully built blue roan. All the other horses moved away when he came near. Next to Buck, he was easily the largest stallion in the valley.

"That's Brutus."

A laugh burst from Cade's throat. "You put a lot of thought into your names."

She laughed, too, the sound high and sweet. "Just calling it like I see it."

And with a lot of accuracy. Cade was surprised to discover he enjoyed being near this woman. She was smart and had a fun sense of humor. She made him laugh, something he hadn't done much of in a long time.

"I used to think about starting up an outfitters business in the area," he confided. "I thought I could serve as a guide for people who want to ride and take pack horses deep into the mountains to view the wilderness areas."

"Why haven't you done it?"

He threw the last piece of his sandwich to Gus, who caught it midair. "I figured it would take me away from my medical office too much."

"Maybe you should think about it again," she suggested.

"Yeah, maybe I should." But he wouldn't. Though

he loved traveling into the high mountains, doing it all the time, for a living, didn't seem to fit with what the Lord wanted him to do. Instead, he felt as though God wanted him to stay near town where he could serve others with his medical degree.

Once the bighorn sheep had taken their fill of water, they moved up the canyon on the other side of the creek and disappeared from view. Seeming agitated by the scent of people so close to their location, the herds of horses gradually left, until only Buck's band remained.

"I still haven't seen the black filly." Even Cade was starting to worry about the foal and her dam.

"Let's go down and take a look, shall we?" Lyn stood and brushed off her pants before gathering up the remnants of their meal and stowing the trash inside her saddlebags.

She stepped up on her horse. Cade joined her, admiring her fluid grace. He didn't know many women who rode as well as Lyn, even more surprising since she didn't own a horse and refused to let Kristen ride.

Down beside the stream, she shook her head in disgust. "The sedges and willows are almost gone. Nothing but mud here. Notice all the horse tracks around?"

He nodded, wishing the horses hadn't done this damage. But he'd seen it with his own eyes and couldn't deny it. "What plants should be growing here?"

"Sedges and Great Basin wild rye are key to a healthy meadow. They're also more fire resistant because they stay green longer than cheatgrass. Without willows, there's no overhang along the creek to protect the fish and their spawning beds. The water gets too warm for eggs to hatch, so the fish die off."

"You got any cattle feeding up here?" He wanted to make sure cows weren't helping cause this problem.

"Nope. We haven't allowed grazing permittees in this area for six years. This is all wild horse–caused damage, and it needs to be repaired soon."

His gaze combed the torn-up slopes of the banks where the horses had decimated every bit of plant life and were now destroying the creek.

"Can we do something about it without removing any of the mustangs?" he asked.

"We can definitely seed the area with healthy plants, but the horses would eat it down before it could gain any growth. We can either remove some of the mustangs or fence off the area. And I don't have the budget for building a fence. It's cheaper to call in the BLM to remove some of the horses than it is to build a fence that the horses can break through."

His heart plunged. "Surely the taxpayers can contribute to keeping the wild horses free. The mustangs are a symbol of our national heritage."

Lyn paused as though choosing her words carefully. "*All* of these animals are part of our national heritage. Not just the horses. The public does pay taxes, but the funds only go so far. For some people, this problem becomes an emotional issue, not a rational, ecological issue. I have to remain impartial and do what is right, even if I think a wild horse with a cute little foal is more appealing than a brown Angus cow. Our nation needs them both, Cade. We can't let the horses destroy things any more than we can let the cows and sheep overgraze the land. Something must be done to mediate this problem."

His shoulders tensed. He'd received a harsh lesson today. He'd been so certain the horses couldn't be doing any harm. Learning he was wrong was a difficult pill to swallow. Lyn had shown him things he'd never noticed before. Educating him in a way he wasn't sure he wanted to accept.

"The horses used to run free across this nation. There wasn't any problem then. What changed?" he asked.

Lyn loosened her grip on the reins, speaking in a soothing voice. "Man is here. We now have towns, cities and highways all across the land. Are you going to tell thousands of people they can't live in our towns because their houses and businesses are in the way of the mustangs?"

"No, of course not."

"That's right. So in the meantime, we have to manage the resources we still have available. And that includes the wild horses. Why should they be treated any differently just because they're prettier than a cow or an elk? We eat cows and hunt elk, but no one hunts horses. No matter what we do, some of the mustangs will need to be moved off this range."

No! Not another roundup. Not if he could stop it.

Her words hung in the air like frost. He didn't respond. Not when he couldn't argue with her reasoning. But his stomach tightened when he thought of rounding up the mares and new foals. Young and weak horses sometimes died during roundups. The mustangs got separated from their family herds. He couldn't stand for that to happen.

He was quiet as they rode back in the opposite direction from which they'd come. Neither one spoke much, both lost in their own thoughts. And that's when he saw the ravens, flying in a cluster over a deep gully ahead of them. Flash's ears pricked forward. Gus paused, then issued a series of staccato barks. Lyn's mare jigged to the side, head up and nostrils flared. All the animals sensed something wrong.

"What do you think it is?" Lyn asked.

"Carrion. Those ravens are getting ready for dinner."

Lyn released a deep sigh of apprehension. "Let's go take a look, but be cautious. I don't carry a gun."

"I do."

She jerked her head around to look at him, obviously surprised by his admission.

"Don't worry. It's legal," he said. "I only carry it for protection. You can't be too careful out here in the wilderness. Lots of bears and mountain lions."

She seemed to accept his explanation. He admired her courage, working in these mountains without a way to protect herself. Against his resolve not to, he liked her more and more.

As they galloped across the expanse of sagebrush, he realized he'd enjoyed this outing even if he didn't like the outcome. He'd learned that Lyndsy Warner was an intelligent, compassionate woman.

Surely they could come up with a better resolution than moving the mustangs. The Toyakoi Tribe wasn't prepared to tolerate a wild-horse roundup without trying to thwart it.

And that meant going up against Lyn. Something Cade now dreaded.

Chapter Five

A hoarse squeal echoed through the canyon, filled with pain and fear. Startled by the horrible sound, Lyn jerked on the reins. Apple jittered among the loose gravel on the incline, resisting Lyn's command to walk forward. Cade's horse acted much the same, tugging on the reins as the flock of ravens darted through the air, almost directly overhead.

Only Gus acted eager to see what was in the gully. He plowed ahead, picking his way over the sharp rocks, his tail high. Though she dreaded what they might find, Lyn stepped off Apple and tied the horse securely to the skeletal remains of a juniper tree. Cade did likewise, neither one of them speaking as they walked the rest of the way down the ravine.

"Gus, stay." Cade pointed at the dog, who immediately sat, gazing at the scene with intelligent eyes.

On the floor of the gulch, a chestnut mare lay on her side on the sunbaked earth. Her coat gleamed with sweat and blood. White saliva frothed at her mouth, her duress palpable in her wheezing breaths. She squealed in agony, a deep, wrenching sound that nearly broke Lyn's heart.

The cause was easy to discern. The mare's right front leg had received a compound fracture. The horse couldn't rise and walk no matter how hard she tried. Without intervention, she would die a long, cruel death.

The black foal with the white tail and mane stood close beside her dam. The filly's tiny squeals indicated her alarm as she nuzzled her mother's face.

"What must have happened?" Lyn breathed the words, taking in the situation with one glance. No wonder she hadn't seen the foal and her mother among the other horses in the valley.

"The mare probably stepped in a hole and broke her leg," Cade murmured, his voice tight with empathy. "Possibly evading a predator, or simply galloping across this bumpy ground. One misstep can mean life or death out here."

Together, they approached the downed horse. The animal thrashed about, trying valiantly to rise but falling back to the ground in an exhausted heap. She nickered to her baby, her breath coming in shallow puffs.

"There, momma," Lyn soothed. "We only want to help."

The filly skittered away, but soon returned. Too young to fully understand the potential danger. Desperate for the protection of her mother.

While Cade knelt beside the injured horse, Lyn easily caught and looped her arms around the neck of the foal. The baby immediately quieted, her breath rushing through her lungs in an anxious exhale. Too immature to know Lyn was human and that she should fight for her freedom. Without help, the baby would die.

"Is there anything you can do?" Lyn spoke softly to Cade, trying not to upset the mustangs any more than they already were.

Cade's face looked drained and pale. He didn't speak for several moments, then answered quietly, "Yes. There's something I can do."

Without explanation, he stood and walked up the hill to Flash. He was a medical doctor, but Lyn doubted a first-aid kit would do any good with this injury. It looked like a serious break. Though he wasn't a veterinarian, she had confidence Cade knew what to do. Surely he could help the mare. He might even be able to set the bone, but how could they get the mare out of here? And where should they take the mustang until her leg could heal?

He returned with a handgun.

Lyn swallowed hard, understanding his intention. She didn't know what kind of gun it was, or the caliber of bullet, but only that it was used for killing.

He placed his hand on her shoulder. She felt the warmth of his touch through her shirt, along with the heavy weight resting on his heart. He met her gaze and she saw sadness in his eyes, along with a firm resolution of what needed to be done.

"I'm sorry, Lyn. There's no other way. The break is too severe. Even if I could set the leg, the mare is wild and would never let it heal. She'd have to stay off it for weeks. I can't leave her here to suffer or be eaten alive by ravens and coyotes."

"I agree." She nodded, ignoring the tears streaming down her face. She was too uncertain of her voice to speak right now. And she felt utterly helpless and ridiculous because she was being so emotional.

Instead, she pulled the foal into her arms and settled on the ground, holding the baby tight. She could hear Cade's footsteps as he returned to the mare, like a plodding death march. Could hear the powerful beating of her own heart pounding in her ears.

She looked up and saw Cade standing over the mare, the pistol held tightly in one hand. He loosened the top two buttons of his shirt and took a deep breath. His face drained of all color, and his eyes filled with grief. Lyn caught a glimpse of the scar on his throat and another one snaking upward across his chest.

Then he turned away. Setting the weapon aside, he knelt next to the mare and closed his eyes. As he rested his hands on his upper thighs, his lips moved in a silent prayer. For several moments, his features were torn by reverence and anguish. Then he arose and picked up the gun.

Lyn pressed her face against the warm coat of the quivering foal. She held her breath. Waiting.

The sound of the gunshot echoed off the canyon walls. Both Lyn and the filly jerked. Lyn's entire being filled with gloom.

Everything went still. Quiet. No sounds, no movements of birds or trees or wind. Only an eerie calm that heralded the loss of life.

The anguish of the dying mare silenced immediately. Peace settled over the earth, but not within Lyn's soul.

Lifting her head, she studied Cade. He stood over the silent mare, his arms by his sides, the gun held limp in his long fingers. He stared at the wild mustang, his face void of expression. But in his eyes, Lyn saw wrenching torment. Something that could only be described as self-loathing.

He'd had to kill one of the wild mustangs he loved.

Cade looked out at the desolate gully. It mirrored his eyes. Nothing but numbing sadness. And then he lifted the weapon he'd used and glared at it with revulsion. He threw it aside in the dirt, as though it were a vile thing that had contaminated him.

But it was too late. Lyn knew without asking. For just these few moments in time, Cade stood exposed. Vulnerable.

Knowing he was a marine, she couldn't help wondering if he'd killed before, in the act of war. Men who'd been declared his enemy, but were still human beings with the same Creator. What had Cade survived? She could only guess. And her heart went out to him, for all he'd suffered. For all he'd lost.

She didn't move. Not for several heart-pounding minutes, until Cade returned. He knelt beside her, wrapping one arm around her back. Patting her shoulder.

Comforting her.

She leaned against him, taking what he offered. Sharing a moment with him that she'd never experienced with anyone before. A closeness she couldn't comprehend.

So much for not becoming friends.

"You okay?" His voice sounded weary. As though the weight of a thousand dying souls rested on his heart.

She nodded, not yet trusting her voice.

"I'm sorry you had to witness this. So sorry," he said.

She felt the warmth of his breath against her cheek and closed her eyes. She was beyond grateful he'd been with her today so she didn't have to face this alone. She had no idea what she might have done if Cade hadn't been here. Without a gun, she would have been forced to leave the mare to die alone. And that knowledge would have torn at her the rest of her life.

She looked up, so close to him that she could see the tenderness in his eyes. The compassion. Even in his own sorrow, he was more concerned for her. What kind of man was Cade Baldwin? She no longer knew.

An odd fluttering filled her chest. A craving to be more than friends with this man. But that was impossible. Wasn't it? And yet they were. Not friends, but something more. Something deeper that she couldn't explain.

"I…I'll be fine." She pulled back, refusing to look again at the dead mare.

He offered his hand as she stood, and she felt the rough calluses on his palms. She left the foal in his care while she returned to her horse and retrieved a long length of rope from her saddlebags. She took her time, trying to still the trembling of her limbs and the stutter of her heart. When she gained her composure, she returned and found Cade standing near the mare with his canteen. As though he couldn't bear to abandon the dead horse.

Now Lyn became the comforter. Avoiding looking at the mare, she went to Cade and touched his arm, knowing he felt the same as her. The helpless frustration that there was no way to change this outcome. Death was a part of life, but it was never pleasant or easy.

"You did the right thing," she said.

He looked at her, his eyes dry but glazed with torment. It was as if he'd been transported somewhere else in time. Back to Afghanistan maybe?

"I never wanted to hurt anyone. All I ever wanted to be was a doctor. To help people," he said.

Surely he was talking about the war. His voice cracked, and so did her heart. Her respect for him grew. Even a big, strong man like Dr. Baldwin couldn't remain detached when faced with the suffering of these innocent animals.

"Come on. It's time for us to go." She tugged on his arm, and he went with her up the hill.

Cade's eyes cleared, and he seemed to return to the present all at once. "We can't leave yet."

He nodded at the filly. Together, they gazed at the baby. Abandoning the little horse here alone was just as cruel as leaving its mother to suffer in death. By nightfall, the foal would undoubtedly become prey to coyotes, mountain lions, or dehydration and death.

The filly didn't blink, looking at them with large, brown eyes. Soft and clear. Filled with trust. Lyn knew what she must do, but every piece of decency within her rebelled.

"I'm supposed to leave her here. I'm not supposed to interfere with wildlife like this," she mumbled, unable to take her gaze off the black beauty. Hating the thought of abandoning the baby.

"Even with a helpless foal?" he asked.

"That's right. I'm supposed to leave her alone and let nature take its course."

He took a step. "She'll die without her momma. You know that."

"Yes, I know."

"You interfere with the wildlife when you build fences or round up horses to remove them from the range. We just interfered with the mare. Why can't you help an orphaned foal?"

He was right, of course. And as much as she respected the dictates of her job, Lyn couldn't let this happen. She'd already made up her mind. She just hoped Cade would agree to what she planned.

With little work, she tied a bowline knot and slid the rope around the filly's neck. Not too tight to choke the baby horse, but tight enough that she couldn't get away. The foal didn't fight Lyn, merely flicking her miniature tail.

"Cade, I have a proposition for you," Lyn said as she worked.

"And what's that?" He stood close by, watching

her with a bit of misgiving. Hadn't he ever seen a woman tie a bowline knot before?

"You have lots of corrals and a fine barn with plenty of room. I live in a Forest Service house in the middle of town. I can't keep the filly with me, but I'll pay you for her upkeep. Would you mind keeping the foal and taking care of her out at your place until I can arrange to buy her from the BLM?"

Lyn looked at him, conveying her desperate request with every fiber of her being.

"Of course I'll keep her, but you don't need to pay me. I'll do it gladly."

"Thank you." She breathed with relief.

With the matter decided between them, they didn't discuss it further. Lyn walked across the washout to collect Cade's discarded gun. She couldn't leave it out here for someone to find. She'd return it to him later, after he'd recovered from today's events.

Her feet sank deep into the sandy waste. Her calf muscles burned with the exertion, but it gave her a moment to gather her wits. Out of her peripheral vision, she saw Cade as he led the filly back to their horses.

Within minutes, they were riding toward the canyon where they'd parked the Forest Service truck. Cade's voice sounded almost normal when he called Gus to join them. The dog trotted along beside them, herding the foal from behind when it tugged stubbornly against the pull of the rope.

Lyn didn't care to talk and noticed from his silence that Cade felt the same. A leaden cloud of sadness rested over them, dampening them with gloom.

At their base, they loaded the horses in the trailer and crowded Gus and the filly into the front of the truck with them. If they put the baby in the back with the adult horses, she might be injured. They had no choice but to keep her with them, and Cade did his best to keep her quiet. Only when they were driving down the mountain did Lyn stop to think that Cade could get her fired if he told the forest supervisor that she'd taken a wild foal home with her. Lyn thought about pleading with Cade to keep his silence, but didn't. She needed her livelihood, but she needed her humanity even more. Saving the filly had been the right thing to do. She'd work it out with the BLM somehow.

She just hoped Cade wasn't a vindictive man.

Cade couldn't stop trembling like a little kid. Yes, he'd done the right thing by putting the mare down, but pulling the trigger had left him bereft and shaking. For several moments, he'd been transported back in time to the war in Afghanistan. To the sounds of bullets spraying against buildings and the bodies of screaming men.

People he knew so well. Friends he'd cared about. So much death. So much blood.

Then he'd felt Lyn Warner's touch on his arm, gentling him the way she'd gentled the orphaned foal. Soothing his raw nerves. Bringing him back to the present.

He'd never forget the anguish on Lyn's face after he'd killed the mare. Her soft sob as she held tight to the filly, whispering that everything would be okay. Speaking to the little horse as though it was a newborn infant and depended on her for survival. And then her quiet request that he keep the foal out at his ranch.

No, this woman wasn't at all like the coarse forest rangers Cade had dealt with in the past. But neither did he believe he could take advantage of her where the mustangs were concerned. She had compassion for the wild horses, but she would still do what she believed was right.

She'd still call for a wild-horse roundup when the time came.

The hour-long drive down the mountain seemed to take only seconds. Cade had his hands full keeping the baby horse quiet. Back at Cade's ranch, they unloaded Flash and took the filly to the barn. At his urging, Lyn took a pitchfork and spread fresh straw in a clean stall. It'd be warm when the foal bedded down for the night.

Cade took a clean bucket and disappeared for a

short time. When he returned, he opened a cabinet and took out a large feeding bottle his grandfather had used to wean baby calves. It'd been a long time since Cade had seen the process, and he tried to remember what Grandfather had taught him. If the filly refused to drink, she'd die.

Cade poured the contents from the bucket into the bottle, noticing Lyn's gaze resting on him with curiosity.

"Where did you get the milk?" she asked.

He didn't look at her. "I have a goat. If we want the foal to survive, it's critical that she eat soon. This meal will tide her over while I drive into town for some milk replacer and foal pellets. She'll need to eat four times a day until I can determine how much hay she's eating. Later, I'll introduce her to Nannie and hope they get along."

"Nannie?"

"My nanny goat. If they like each other, then the filly needn't be left all alone. I don't dare put the foal with Flash until she's much older. He might hurt her. But I also have a gentle old mare who might take to the baby horse for companionship. We'll have to see."

Inside the warm stall, he petted the tremulous foal's neck, letting the baby suck two of his fingers. With his fingers still in the filly's mouth, he inserted the nipple and let hunger be the guide.

No urging was needed. The horse sucked noisily, tugging on the bottle, voracious with hunger. Lyn stood close by, petting the filly's back with approval.

"What a good girl," she said.

Cade held the bottle with both hands so the horse wouldn't pull it free. "I'm not sure how long her mother was down. It's probably been a while since the filly's been able to eat."

"I'll bet she's starving."

"No doubt. But I don't want to overfeed her and give her intestinal problems. That could be just as deadly."

The foal jerked against the bottle. Cade drew back, caught off guard. He stumbled before he caught himself.

"Hey, little girl. Mind your manners," he scolded playfully.

Lyn laughed, the sound warming Cade's heart like nothing else could. Having her here helped ease the trauma of the day, and he was glad to share this successful feeding with her.

"Thanks for this." Lyn paused in rubbing the baby's ears as she smiled up at him.

"No, thank you. This has been a very…unexpected day."

"It sure has." She looked toward the barn door. "I'll unload Flash for you while you feed the foal."

Without waiting for his approval, she turned and walked out into the sunlight. Minutes later, she was

back with his saddle, grunting as she hefted it over
the saddle rack. She was certainly no sissy girl who
needed a man to do everything for her.

"Flash is happily drinking water and nibbling at
hay," she said softly.

"Thanks." He tilted the near-empty bottle so the
foal could drain every last drop.

"If you tell me what to buy, I can drive into town
for the milk supplement," she offered.

"That won't be necessary. I'll take good care of
her, don't worry. In fact, you should bring Kristen
out sometime. Maybe she can name the foal. But
wait a few days, until the baby gets over the stress
of losing her momma and having a new home."

"I'm sure Kristen would like that a lot. There's
nothing in the world she loves more than horses."

She stood there watching him until the bottle
was empty. They seemed to have run out of things
to say, and he glanced at her, feeling out of place
in his own barn.

"Well, I guess I'd best get going," Lyn said. "I'll
call before I bring Kristen out next week."

"Thanks again. It was an enlightening day, but
I'm sure glad it's almost over."

"Me, too. It's certainly not a day I'll soon forget," she agreed.

He nodded, watching through the dim shadows of the barn as Lyn pivoted on her boot heels
and walked away. He ran his hands over the filly,

speaking calming words. The sounds of an engine and tires grating across his gravel driveway met his ears. He waited until all quieted, then walked outside.

Lyn's truck and trailer were just disappearing over the hill, heading back to town. Cade breathed a deep sigh, trying to sort out his emotions. He'd shared a cruel and amazing experience with the forest ranger. Somehow it'd brought them closer together. And yet, it'd also driven them further apart.

He couldn't explain how he felt about Lyn or this odd situation he found himself in. The baby horse didn't change anything between them. Not really. He had a job to do, and so did Lyn. Cade planned to save the wild horses if he could. And nothing must stand in the way of that.

Not even an orphaned baby horse.

Chapter Six

"What are you thinking about so intently?" The following Wednesday, Lyn leaned against the doorjamb to her kitchen and gazed at her daughter. Kristen sat in a chair at the table, staring out the window at the wide, empty street where they lived. It was the anniversary of the car accident, and both of them had been feeling melancholy all day. Lyn had taken the day off work and let Kristen stay home from school. Neither of them felt like doing much.

Kristen turned her head away and brushed a hand across her eyes, but not before Lyn saw the shimmer of tears. Twin furrows permanently lined Kristen's forehead, an oddity for such a young child. Life had not been kind to this little girl, and Lyn was amazed Kristen had adjusted as well as she had.

"I'm not thinking about anything." The child's voice quivered with emotion.

Lyn knew better, but decided not to push the issue. She didn't want to start another fight. Many times she caught Kristen staring blankly out the window as though she'd been transformed to another place and time. Sometimes Kristen watched the neighbor kids as they ran around their yard and played with their dog. Other times Kristen studied the empty road, as if expecting someone to appear. But no one came. Just a vacant void that seemed to mirror her heart.

Lyn glanced at the science book and papers spread across the table. Dressed in warm sweatpants, Kristen had read several chapters ahead, having already completed the homework she would turn in to her teacher tomorrow morning.

Bored and lonely. Anyone could see that Kristen was unhappy. Even her teacher remarked on it during her parent-teacher conference last week. And yet, Kristen continued to excel in school. Because she'd promised her dad before the accident that she'd always work hard in her studies. Now that Rob was gone, Kristen took that promise seriously. It was the last pledge the girl could keep to her father.

Lyn bit her bottom lip to keep from asking questions she knew Kristen didn't want to answer. How was she feeling? Was she missing her daddy today? Did she want to talk about it? Would she like a bowl of chocolate ice cream?

Such questions tended to make the girl angry. She didn't want to talk about anything. Not with anyone. Neither did Lyn. Still, she couldn't help wishing Kristen would confide in her. Since the accident, it seemed a giant gulf had sprung up between them. And deep inside her heart, Lyn feared the reason was because Kristen blamed her for the accident.

Just like Lyn blamed herself.

"How'd you like to do something really fun this afternoon?" Lyn asked, trying to sound enthusiastic.

Kristen pursed her lips with skepticism. "No."

"How can you say no without knowing what it is?"

"I don't want to go look at more pine trees."

Lyn laughed. "We aren't going to look at a timber stand. This will be fun for *you*."

"What is it?" No eagerness filled her words.

Walking to the hall closet, Lyn reached inside for their warm jackets. Leaden clouds filled the afternoon sky, and the cool spring day smelled of rain. "You'll see. But I guarantee you'll like it."

The frown marring Kristen's forehead eased just a bit. Lyn didn't pursue more conversation as she helped the girl put on her prosthetic leg. Together, they walked outside to the car. On the porch steps, Kristen stumbled and would have gone sprawling if Lyn hadn't grabbed her arm.

"I'm okay. I want to do it myself. Dr. Baldwin says it's okay if I fall." Kristen shrugged off Lyn's hand and clasped the railing tight.

Lyn forced herself to stand back and watch as Kristen sidestepped down the stairs one at a time. She didn't agree that it was all right if the girl fell. Kristen could be seriously injured. Over time, Cade would hopefully help her daughter become steadier on stairs.

"Where we going?" the girl asked as they drove down Main Street.

"You'll see."

A feeling of expectancy overwhelmed Lyn. Cade knew they were coming. The filly was doing well, and he thought it was time they gave the horse a name. The fact that he wanted to let Kristen have that honor left Lyn feeling grateful for his thoughtfulness.

"I'd rather stay home," Kristen said. "I don't want to look at a bunch of sagebrush today."

Lyn chuckled. "We're not going to look at sage, other than during the drive to our destination."

"Where are we going?"

"I told you. It's a surprise. But you won't want to miss out on this, believe me."

"Hmm." The girl harrumphed and flounced around to glare out her window, not at all interested in what her mother wanted to show her.

Lyn couldn't blame her. So many times she'd

dragged Kristen with her into the mountains or out to look at a lake. Too many times to count. Her work demanded it. Lyn couldn't leave Kristen home alone. Normally, kids liked to run and play outdoors, chasing chipmunks and rabbits. But not Kristen. The uneven ground made it more difficult for her to walk, and she usually ended up falling over a rock or tree limb in her path. Lyn was always right there to help her up, despite Kristen's angry insistence that she could do it herself.

But today was different. Kristen would like this surprise.

Lyn hoped.

As they headed outside of town, they passed the redbrick church. The soft chords of organ music and harmonic voices singing a hymn rose through the air. Lyn rolled down her window just an inch to catch the melody better. And then the voice of a soprano sang the high, sweet notes. A song of praise and devotion to God.

Goose bumps dotted her arms as Lyn glimpsed the green, trim lawns edging the church. So quaint and peaceful. A feeling of reverence blanketed her. It'd been so long since she'd attended a church service.

Since before Rob died.

"Why don't we go to church anymore?" Kristen asked.

At first, Lyn was speechless. How could she

explain to her daughter that her heart was deadened toward the Lord? Yes, Lyn still believed in God, but she was also very angry at Him. If He loved them, if He really cared, then why had He taken her husband and let something so horrible happen to dear, innocent Kristen?

"I...we've been so busy, with you in the hospital and then our transfer here to Stokely. There hasn't been a lot of extra time."

"We don't pray anymore, either," the girl persisted.

Lyn rolled up her window, avoiding her daughter's penetrating gaze. On the one hand, she wanted to teach her child about God. To set a good example of service, devotion and faith. But on the other hand, how could Lyn be something she didn't feel inside?

Maybe you should change that.

The thought filled Lyn's mind. But how? How could she feel at peace after all that had happened? After all they'd been through?

She'd avoided this issue for so long. Ignoring God and working on Sundays had become an easy habit. Easier than getting up and taking her amputee child to church. But now, Kristen was old enough to understand. She'd started asking questions about life and death and where her daddy had gone. And Lyn didn't feel prepared to answer appropriately. How could she tell her child something she didn't know if she believed herself?

You should find out.

The thought filled Lyn's mind, and she felt the weight of responsibility to her daughter resting heavily on her shoulders.

"Maybe we can pray more often," she said.

"It doesn't matter. God doesn't love us anyway," Kristen said.

Hearing her own feelings spoken out loud struck Lyn's heart like a physical blow. Everything within her rebelled. She opened her mouth to dispute Kristen's claim, but couldn't say the words. And yet, it went against everything Lyn had been brought up to believe and trust in. Maybe it wasn't fair for her to withhold the strengthening element of God from her daughter just because she harbored resentment toward the Lord. If ever they needed God's help, it was now.

But where was God the night of the car accident? And where was He when the doctors decided to take Kristen's leg?

Maybe Lyn had ignored her anger long enough. But she didn't know how to become closer to the Lord when she wanted nothing to do with Him.

Pray. That was the answer. Lyn knew it without a doubt. But it was more than difficult to pray to a God she felt anger toward.

"I don't believe God doesn't love us." Lyn spoke the words woodenly.

"Then why'd He take Daddy away?"

"I don't know. I can only hope He had a good reason," Lyn answered truthfully, relieved when Kristen let the subject drop.

As they pulled into the yard at Sunrise Ranch, she pushed aside her misgivings and decided to focus on Kristen today. Making her daughter happy was all that mattered now. Kristen was her whole life. But God was waiting for them, Lyn knew. Waiting for them to return to Him.

"That's Dr. Baldwin." Kristen pointed at Cade, who stood out in the middle of the corral, wearing a pair of leather gloves and holding a tin bucket.

He looked toward them, squinting against the sun, tugging the brim of his battered cowboy hat lower across his eyes. He looked so handsome, standing there dressed in faded denims and a white T-shirt tucked into his pants. Beside him stood a gray-and-white goat. The black filly raced past, kicking up her heels and flicking her white tail. Filled with energy and life.

"Look, Mom. A baby horse. She moves like lightning," Kristen exclaimed.

The girl thrust the car door open and swiveled around in her seat. Bracing her hands against the dashboard and the back of the seat, she stood and was out of the car so fast that Lyn had no opportunity to help her.

Wow! This was a first.

Holding on to the door for support, Kristen settled her hips over the prosthesis so she could walk. She'd navigated past the shifting gravel and reached the rail fence by the time Lyn was able to take hold of her arm.

Cade sauntered over to greet them, a wide smile on his handsome face. "Hi, there, ladies. You want to see the new filly?"

Kristen's head bobbed up and down. Disengaging her mother's hand, she clopped forward over the clumps of grass bordering the corral. Cade met her at the gate. Lyn couldn't remember seeing her daughter so eager and light of foot since the accident.

"Why is the baby horse with a goat? Where's the baby's momma? Can I pet them? Do goats bite? I wish I had a horse. I love horses. How many do you have? My dad rode horses. We were gonna buy one once, but we had the accident instead. Is Gus your only dog?" Kristen sprayed questions at Cade like a machine gun sprays bullets.

The next corral over, an old gray mare stood with her head over the top rail. Her ears pricked forward as she watched the group with interest. Lyn couldn't see Flash.

Cade lifted the rope tie for the corral to admit

them inside. "Gus is my only dog. The filly doesn't have a mom. She's an orphan. So I'm feeding her goat's milk until I wean her on to hay. I have two horses and a goat. Flash, Magpie and the goat's name is Nannie. This goat doesn't bite, but others might." He pointed at the gray mare. "That's Magpie. I'm hoping she'll make friends with the filly so I can put them together once the baby gets a little bigger. I'm sure your dad was a great man. And yes, you can pet the filly. But first, let me put this bucket of milk down where it won't get spilled. Then you can help me feed her."

Lyn's head whirled with so many questions and answers, but Kristen seemed to keep up just fine.

"I get to help?" The girl's eyes glowed with happiness, her face and gestures animated.

Finally. Finally Lyn had found something harmless that Kristen could enjoy without getting hurt. Finally, she'd done something right without earning the displeasure of her daughter.

"Come on. I'll let you help me get the bottle ready." Cade winked at Lyn before disappearing with Kristen inside the barn.

Watching the kind doctor interact with her daughter brought Lyn a great deal of comfort. This visit to Sunrise Ranch would do Kristen some good. But in the back of her mind, Lyn realized a lot of issues remained unresolved. Such as what to do about the wild horses without losing Cade's friendship. And how to mend her relationship with God.

But right now, those problems would have to wait.

Cade could hardly contain his excitement. For several days, he'd anticipated Lyn's visit like a child waiting for Christmas morning. And he didn't understand why. So he could be close by in case the filly needed him, he'd had his receptionist reschedule appointments at his doctor's office this week. Other than the filly's progress, today was nothing special. No big deal.

And yet, it was.

Now that she was here, he watched Kristen carefully to see how she was progressing with her walking and morale. This visit would be good for the little girl. Hopefully, it'd be good for her mother, too.

The clean aroma of hay filled the warm barn. Kristen followed him over to a large cabinet where he took out a sterile feeding bottle. He showed her how to mix the milk formula while Lyn brought in the eager filly.

Lyn shook her head in awe. "I can't believe how much she's grown."

"Yes, she's got a huge appetite," Cade agreed with a chuckle.

"Oh, she's so pretty." Kristen's voice quivered with bliss.

The little horse jerked up her head, nostrils flared.

"Did I scare you, baby?" Kristen whispered, and petted the filly. "I'll talk more softly. You don't ever need to be afraid of me. I'd never hurt you. Not in a zillion years. We're gonna be best friends, okay?"

The foal pricked her ears forward, her large, brown eyes filled with warmth and intelligence.

The first attempt at feeding the impatient foal ended with Kristen being knocked backward into the soft straw. The girl lay there in wide-eyed surprise for several seconds.

"Kristen! Are you okay?" Lyn hurried to help her daughter up, her worried gaze scanning the girl for signs of injury.

Cade held his breath, hoping they didn't blow this out of proportion. Lyn seemed to be two different people. When they rode up on the mountain, she was calm and collected. Proficient and reasonable. But when it came to Kristen, she became clingy and controlling. Downright fearful.

Cade hadn't told Lyn, but inviting Kristen out here today was a form of therapy for the child. Now he realized Lyn also needed healing. To trust and let go. If they didn't react positively, he'd have to try another strategy.

Kristen giggled and sat up. "I'm fine, Mom."

At least one of them was responding well.

The girl used the stall to brace herself so she could stand. Lyn tried to help, but Kristen brushed her aside. "I can do it, Mom. Don't help me."

Yes! This was what Cade was looking for. An assertion of independence.

"If you need help, just ask," he said.

Lyn stood back, her gaze wary and alert as Kristen reached for the bottle again. The girl showed no anger or tears, but only infinite patience as she offered the little horse the bottle. "Let's try this again. I know how it feels to be so hungry you can't hardly wait."

"Remember to hold tight. This is a famished baby." Cade ignored Lyn's look of dismay. He was delighted Kristen wasn't nervous around the filly. If only he could get Lyn to loosen up, they'd be all right.

Kristen gripped the bottle, her gaze fogged by joy as she focused on the filly. "She's so beautiful. Mostly all black with a white tail and mane. I've never seen such a pretty horse in all my life."

"I agree." Cade laughed, knowing the girl was completely enamored by the little foal. Good. She needed something to feel happy about. Something positive and fun.

"So what will you name her?" Lyn asked.

Cade met Lyn's eyes with approval. They'd planned this moment beforehand. He couldn't think of better therapy for a girl in Kristen's situation.

Kristen went very still. The loud squeaking sounds of the baby filled the air as she sucked on the bottle to get every drop of milk. "I can name her?"

"Yes, in fact, she's yours," Cade said.

Kristen gasped with pleasure. "Mine? All mine? Really?"

"Yes, really." Why had he said that? He hadn't planned to give the horse to Kristen. Not without asking her mother first. But the words just poured out of his mouth. He couldn't take them back now. Not unless Lyn refused his offer.

The smile on Lyn's face dropped like stone. "Cade, we didn't discuss this. I…we can't keep a horse."

"Don't worry. She'll stay right here. Kristen can visit anytime she likes." He tried to sound positive. By agreeing to keep the filly at Sunrise Ranch, Cade was trying to make it easy for Lyn to accept. To relax and let Kristen mentally adopt the foal. To have something of her own.

"But I—"

"Oh, thank you, Dr. Baldwin!" Kristen whirled about and threw her arms around his waist, hugging tight.

Lyn stood staring at them in confusion, her hands balled into tight fists. Her face mottled red with frustration. Over the top of Kristen's head, he met Lyn's eyes and mouthed the words, "Don't worry. It's gonna be okay."

To which Lyn closed her eyes for the count of two and took a deep inhale. Good. This wasn't easy on Lyn, either, but she was learning to cope.

Cade tugged himself free and pointed toward Lyn. "Don't thank me. Thank your mother. She's the one who saved the filly after her momma died. This was her idea."

Kristen stared at her mother in surprise. Then she hugged Lyn, her voice filled with adoration. "Oh, thank you, Mom. You knew I always wanted my own horse, and you finally got me one. Thank you so much. You're the best."

Lyn held her daughter close, her face pale. Every ounce of her stiff body language told Cade she didn't want to let her daughter keep the horse. But she didn't say a word, overcoming her own feelings of inadequacy.

Cade stood back and held the now-empty bottle. Over the girl's head, he watched Lyn carefully. She obviously didn't know what to say. But if she refused, she'd risk her daughter's happiness.

As gently as possible, Cade quickly explained to Kristen about finding the filly's dam badly injured and how Lyn had insisted they couldn't leave the foal there to die.

Kristen stared at her mother with amazement. "You saved the baby?"

Lyn's face flushed with color and she nodded, stammering in confusion. "Y-yes, Cade and I saved her. But you have to understand, Kristen. We...we can't keep the horse at our place. You can visit her whenever I have time to drive us out here, but a horse needs a corral and barn, and we don't have either one at our house."

"I understand. She'll get lots bigger and need plenty of room to run." Completely unflustered, Kristen returned to the foal, rubbing the baby's soft muzzle and throat with her hands. "We'll come visit you every day. I'll name you Lightning. Because that's what you looked like when I first saw you racing around the corral. A streak of lightning with your white tail and mane whipping behind you."

"Honey, I don't know if I can bring you out here every day." Lyn sounded nervous. Filled with panic.

"Just visit whenever you can," Cade said.

This news didn't seem to dampen Kristen's spirits in the least. "We'll visit often," she insisted.

Cade hadn't thought about the hardship frequent visits might pose on Lyn. She was a busy, single working mother with a lot of responsibilities. Bringing Kristen out to Sunrise Ranch every day wouldn't be easy. As a medical doctor, he knew the horse would be great therapy for Kristen, but he wasn't so sure it was the right thing for Lyn.

Or him. He should have known better than to

become emotionally attached to his patient and their family, but he really didn't have a choice. Something about Lyn and her daughter had settled inside a vacant space of his heart, and he found himself caring for them on a highly personal level.

"Lightning is a great name," Lyn said, her voice a bit tremulous. She was obviously doing her best to remain positive while fighting her deep-seated fears. For the benefit of her daughter. And that made Cade like her even more.

"Lightning is a perfect name. It fits her well," Cade agreed.

They spent another hour outside, grooming Lightning and letting Kristen enjoy being a carefree kid for what Cade thought must be the first time in a long time.

Finally, they went inside the house for some hot chocolate. Unable to get enough of the animals, Kristen took her cup outside where she sat on the covered porch with Gus and gazed at the corral. Lightning galloped freely around the goat, who chewed a mouthful of hay in serene detachment. Kristen sat chatting to Gus. The dog responded by licking the child's face, which made Kristen giggle.

"She's happy today," Cade observed.

"Yes. I always hoped after we moved to Stokely that she'd make new friends, but I never thought they'd all be animals," Lyn said.

She stood in his kitchen, gazing out the window

at the back of her daughter's head. Never fully removing her eyes from the child. Always hovering close by, just in case.

Cade turned off the stove and came to join her, taking a sip from his own cup. "This is a good beginning."

Lyn inhaled deeply before letting it go. "I haven't heard her laugh this much since…"

She didn't finish her thought, but she didn't have to. Cade knew. Since before Kristen's father died. "As she becomes happy and more confident within herself, she'll make friends at school more easily."

Lyn turned and looked at him, a bit of doubt filling her expressive eyes. "Is that your professional opinion, or just a hunch?"

His smile broadened to a teasing grin. Trying not to let her take the situation too seriously. Trying to help her see that life could be joyful as well as sad. "That's my professional opinion, Lyn. Come on, sit with me in the living room. Kristen's safe enough with Gus."

He didn't touch her as he headed that way, hoping she took his cue. Hoping he didn't have to coax her away from the view of her daughter.

"I wish you'd warned me before you gave the horse to her. I never would have agreed to that," Lyn said.

"I'm sorry. It just kind of happened. I figure the

horse should belong to you. You're the one who saved her life."

"No, we both saved her."

Okay, he could accept that. Because they'd shared something special, he felt close to this woman. And yet, an invisible barrier kept them miles apart.

"I'm happy to keep Lightning here at my place," he said. "Let Kristen keep the horse, Lyn. It won't do her any harm."

"Keeping the filly here will work, unless I get transferred to another town."

He hadn't thought about that. If Lyn moved away, he wouldn't be able to see her and Kristen anymore. And that left him feeling rotten inside. "Let's worry about that when the time comes."

"Okay." But she didn't sound convinced. Not one bit.

A cheery fire burned in the rock fireplace, chasing the subtle chill from the space. Lyn glanced about the tidy room, taking in the evidence of his Shoshone heritage. Woven baskets with intricate designs decorated the walls and tabletops. A comfy leather sofa and high-backed chairs circled the console TV set. A pair of white knee-moccasins with blue and white beading across the supple leather rested in one corner. Braided rag rugs made by *Kaku,* his grandmother, covered the hardwood floors. A striking headdress created by Grandfather, with eagle feathers, ermine and rabbit fur, had been set up on top of a tall armoire. Cade hadn't changed the place much since his grandparents had lived here. He'd always felt at home with the rustic accommodations, but now wondered if Lyn would find the furnishings garish and old-fashioned.

"You have a lovely home. Everything's so beautiful and comfortable," she said.

From the curious warmth in her eyes, he could tell she meant the compliment sincerely.

"Thanks."

She touched the ornate frame of an old picture resting on the mantel beside a set of Scriptures. A pretty Indian maiden with high cheekbones. Her long, black hair flowed over the shoulders of her white rawhide dress ornamented with feathers and beads. "Is this your mother?"

"Yes. She was a Shoshone princess. It caused quite a scandal when she married my father. He was a white man, and my grandparents didn't like him. They wanted her to marry another member of the tribe, but she didn't love him and refused."

"Well, she's beautiful. I'm glad she married for love."

His heart swelled in agreement. "Me, too. She was the most gentle person I ever knew. She loved all God's creatures, big and small. In fact, she was a lot like Kristen."

"My Kristen?"

"Yes. She wasn't afraid to assert her independence. She adored my father in spite of the tribe's disapproval."

"Did your parents ever live here at Sunrise Ranch?"

He shook his head, remembering how he'd overheard a few snippets of conversation between his parents when they didn't know he was listening. "No, they eloped and moved to California where they raised me. But I came here to spend each summer with my grandparents. I don't remember my parents ever stepping foot in this house after they married. Grandfather wouldn't allow it."

"And yet your grandfather accepted you?"

"Yeah, he figured I was innocent of my parents' deception. Not all the members of the tribe agreed. But Grandfather loved me unconditionally. He taught me so much about life, but he never accepted my father."

"I'm sorry to hear that."

"Don't be. My parents were happy and made their own way. And I was content. I never realized I was half Shoshone until I was nine years old, the first summer I came here to meet my grandparents."

If only his folks were here now, he might not feel so lonely. Returning to Sunrise Ranch had brought him a great deal of comfort, and yet he had no one to confide his heart to anymore. No one to love unconditionally.

"Why aren't you married?" she asked.

He shrugged. "I've dated a lot over the years, but being in the Marine Corps and then medical school consumed most of my time. I never developed a serious relationship. I was ambitious and determined to become a doctor, even if it cut into my personal life. Now that I've met my goals, I'd like a family. Unfortunately, my options for romance are rather limited here in Stokely."

Which pulled his thoughts back to Lyn.

She looked away, his admission causing her face to turn a pretty shade of pink. He'd obviously embarrassed her with his candor. She was way too easy to talk to. But now he'd said the words out loud, he realized he'd never made time for love in his life. And maybe he should think about changing that.

"You must be a religious person." She nodded at the Scriptures on the mantel.

"Yes, my folks raised me to love God. But at some point, every person needs to decide what they believe in, regardless of how they were raised. Speaking of which, I haven't seen you and Kristen at church since you moved to town."

She took a sip of hot chocolate. "I don't know if I believe in God anymore. We used to go to church before…before the accident. But I don't need church to feel spiritual."

"And what about Kristen?"

She didn't respond, letting the question hang in the air. He stepped over to the fire, picking up a metal poker to stir the growing flames. The red coals winked at him and he nudged one away from the fire, resting it close to the hearth. Glancing up, he saw that Lyn watched his every move.

"When we make a conscious effort to be near God, it strengthens us," he said. "We all have the light of Christ born within us, but when we pull away and live our lives without worshipping the Lord, our spirituality can cool and even die." He pointed at the now-blackened coal he'd pulled away from the fire, which no longer glowed with heat.

She smiled tolerantly. "You trying to convert me, Dr. Baldwin?"

"No, just pointing out the obvious. Faith and worship can help mend broken hearts. It might do you and Kristen a lot of good."

She set her cup down on a coaster and stood. "Thanks so much for inviting us out today. We needed this so much."

He sensed something more in her words. "Because Kristen's been so unhappy?"

"Yes. You see, today is the anniversary of her daddy's death."

His heart gave a powerful squeeze. "I imagine today is rather difficult for you, too."

She nodded. "It is. But this has been a great experience for Kristen. She hasn't been this happy in a long time. We'd better be going, though."

He could have kicked himself. He'd been trying to help and hoped he hadn't pushed her too hard. As she headed for the door, he followed, reminding himself that Lyn's life wasn't his business. And yet, they'd both confided in each other. He'd told Lyn things he hadn't told anyone else. Still, Kristen was his patient, not Lyn.

Not a beautiful forest ranger.

After promising to give Kristen an update on Lightning at their next doctor's appointment on Tuesday, he hugged her goodbye. Lyn thanked him again, and then they were gone. As Cade watched them pull out of his driveway, he couldn't help feeling empty inside. He didn't want them to leave. Not so soon.

Surely an odd notion.

Kristen wore visible defects upon her body, but Cade had no doubt Lyn was just as scarred on the inside. He longed to help them both heal, but had serious doubts. Especially since he had his own problems to sort out, and carried similar battle wounds on his own heart. Only time would tell.

Chapter Seven

❦

Over the next week, Lyn took Kristen out to Sunrise Ranch twice more to visit Lightning. The filly thrived under Cade's care. And Kristen flourished with Cade's encouragement at physical therapy. Lyn had never seen her daughter so happy. So amenable and easygoing.

"I have another surprise for you," Cade said two weeks later when they went to his office for their weekly therapy session.

Curious, Lyn followed as he led Kristen into a spacious room set up with a red floor mat, steps and support bars.

A wide smile of pleasure crinkled his eyes. "I made this gait room especially for Kristen."

"Thanks, Dr. Baldwin."

But the girl didn't look too impressed. Lyn could understand why. Her exercises weren't easy. When other kids were outside running and taking their legs for granted, Kristen had to exercise just so she could walk by herself. The fact that he'd gone to this trouble impressed Lyn. Cade was a good man, and she couldn't deny it.

For the next hour he worked with Kristen, even letting Lyn assist with a battery of hip squeezes, extensions, lifts and stretches.

"You're getting stronger. I can tell you're doing your exercises at home," he said.

Kristen nodded. "I do them without Mom even having to remind me."

Lyn smiled, proud of her daughter. "That's right. Sometimes I think she exercises too much."

"I have to, so I can run and play soccer," Kristen said.

Lyn didn't respond. In spite of repeatedly telling Kristen no, the girl kept asking her to complete a health questionnaire and sign her soccer application.

And then Cade presented Kristen with her new C-Leg prosthesis. Or rather, two new prosthetics. One for regular walking, and another J-shaped running prosthesis made of flexible carbon fibers for running.

Kristen's eyes gleamed with excitement as Maya, Cade's assistant, showed the girl how to clean the silicon liner of the C-Leg before rolling it onto her stump without air bubbles.

"She won't need that one." Lyn pointed at the running prosthesis.

Kristen blinked, her lips pinched together. "But I want to use it, Mom."

"I can't afford it, honey." Which was true. A state-of-the-art prosthesis like that might cost thousands of dollars. Health insurance wouldn't cover it, and neither could Lyn. Since she didn't believe it was in the best interest of her child to run, fall and possibly get hurt, the expense seemed the easiest out.

"There's no charge for either prosthesis," Cade said. "The J-shape is a new model the Craig Stratich Group is testing out. They're leading specialists in prosthetics and research. This model isn't even available on the market yet. So you'll be one of the first people to use it."

Lyn sucked back a startled gasp. A variety of emotions swamped her all at once. Gratitude for Cade's generosity, pleasure that Kristen got to be one of the first people to try out the new device, and disappointment that he was making this so easy for them. But she was determined not to sign the soccer form. No way.

Kristen gave a delighted bounce. "Really? That's so cool."

"No strings attached?" Lyn couldn't believe it. There had to be a catch.

"No strings attached," Cade confirmed. "If you're

willing to be part of the study, it's free. I'll just ask Kristen a battery of questions each week when she comes in for her physical therapy about how it's working out for her. No charge."

Lyn hesitated. Kristen fingered the shiny curve of the newfangled limb where it sat beside her on the examination table. The girl's jaw locked hard. Stubborn. Determined. As though she dared her mother to try to take the apparatus away from her. And Lyn couldn't do that. Not if it meant that much to her daughter.

"Okay, she can try it out for a while, but I don't know what use a running prosthesis will be to her." Lyn spoke vaguely, not entirely convinced this was the right thing to do.

"I'm gonna play soccer," Kristen announced.

"That'd be a great idea. There's nothing you can't do if you put your mind to it," Cade said.

Wait! What was he doing?

"No. Remember we talked about this? No soccer. We discussed violin or piano lessons instead," Lyn returned.

Kristen's brow darkened with resentment. "I don't want to play the piano. And I hate the violin."

"How can you hate it? You've never even tried it."

"And I'm not going to."

Lyn didn't really want to have this discussion in front of Cade. She couldn't help remembering him telling her about his mother asserting her will and leaving her family in order to marry the man she loved. If she pushed Kristen hard enough, would the girl leave her? Perhaps when she was grown. In the meantime, Lyn had an obligation to be the best parent she could. "We'll talk about this later on at home."

With a disgusted huff, Kristen turned away. Cade remained silent, but Lyn could see from his doubtful expression that he wanted to argue the point. Thankfully he kept his silence.

Lyn hadn't gone out with Cade to view the mustangs since they'd found and brought the baby horse home. She'd been too busy, and she just didn't have the heart to see the wild horses again so soon. And then Lyn got an unexpected phone call. She didn't know who to be angrier at: Kristen for disobeying her, or Cade for encouraging the girl to try whatever she liked.

"Lyn, your daughter's soccer coach is holding for you on line two." Cindy, Lyn's office manager, made the announcement to her late one afternoon.

Heading back to her office following a meeting with Bob MacKay, the district manager of the BLM, Lyn froze in stride. "Her soccer coach?"

"Yeah, and he says it's urgent."

Confused by the meaning of this, Lyn hurried to

her desk and punched the blinking button on her phone console. "This is Lyn Warner."

"Mrs. Warner, this is Dale Cummings. I'm Kristen's soccer coach."

"I don't understand. She doesn't play soccer."

A long pause followed.

"Um, yes, she does. And I'm afraid she's been injured during a practice game."

A wave of fear cracked through Lyn. She couldn't move. Couldn't breathe. A stupor of dread swirled around inside her mind. Kristen wasn't playing soccer. Lyn had said no. So how could her daughter have a soccer coach? Unless...

"It's nothing serious," he went on. "Just a bloody nose, but she'll be fine. We're at the clinic now. Do you think you can come over here to pick her up?"

"Of course. I'll be right there."

Lyn hung up the phone, her body quaking. On autopilot, she grabbed her purse and dashed down the hall. After a quick word to Cindy as to where she was going, she got into her car and tried to obey the speed limit on her mad dash to Cade's clinic.

The rest of the afternoon was an angry blur. Lyn discovered from the coach that Kristen had completed the forms and forged her mother's signature, giving her permission to play soccer. To explain Lyn's absence, Kristen had told her coach that her mom was always working and couldn't make the practices or games.

Lyn didn't know what to think. Her mind fumed, but her heart billowed with pain. She'd always tried to be so supportive of Kristen in all her school activities. No matter what, she never missed a single choir or science presentation. Every evening, she reviewed the girl's homework. She made cupcakes to share with the class on Kristen's birthday and took time off work so she could chaperone field trips. Now, she could barely look at Cade as the doctor reassured her that Kristen would be fine.

As she drove Kristen home an hour later, she felt hurt by her child's deception and embarrassed that she hadn't been attending her games. Until she could get control over her emotions, Lyn didn't dare speak and make the situation worse.

"I'm sorry, Mom." Kristen's voice sounded muffled from the white cotton balls protruding from her nostrils.

Lyn bit her bottom lip, trying to keep her cool. Trying not to yell and scream and cry. Wondering why this was so difficult.

"You lied to me," she said, her voice trembling just a bit. "You told me to pick you up from school an hour later because you were working with Mrs. Wilson on your science project. Not because you'd forged my signature so you could play soccer after I said no."

"I know, Mom. But you wouldn't let me play

otherwise." An edge of bitterness blunted Kristen's tone.

"And this is exactly why I said no. You got hurt today. Thankfully it was just a bloody nose. But what if it'd been more? What if you'd gotten a concussion, or worse?" A fire of apprehension sparked inside her.

"But I didn't. I scored the winning goal, Mom." The girl's impassioned voice filled the car. "I wish you'd seen me. I can run fast on my J-Leg prosthesis. Faster than any of the other kids. I'm not just the crippled girl anymore. Everyone wants me on their team. I have friends. They all like me now."

And Lyn could just imagine how important that must be to her daughter. To be appreciated and accepted. To be wanted. But Kristen didn't realize her own mortality. Lyn couldn't take chances like this. She couldn't survive another tragedy like the last one. Kristen was all she had left. If something else bad happened, Lyn would never forgive herself.

The way she hadn't forgiven herself for her part in Rob's death.

"If you'd just come see me run, I know you'd understand," Kristen said. "I'm fast. It's like I'm no longer an amputee kid. Because of Dr. Baldwin, I have my leg back."

Regardless of Kristen's disobedience, Lyn was impressed. Kristen was so resilient. She'd taken the running prosthesis and learned to run fast on it in such a short time. Very remarkable. And they had Cade to thank for it.

But it didn't change Lyn's mind.

"No. I don't want to hear another word about it. I've spoken to your coach and you're not playing soccer anymore, and that's final."

Lyn glanced at her daughter. The girl was visibly shaking, her face harsh with rage. But she didn't say another word. Lyn sensed that Kristen was much like an atomic bomb—silent and deadly. Just awaiting a fuse so she could blow.

When they got home, the girl hopped out of the car so fast, Lyn couldn't even keep up. And that's when she noticed how well Kristen was walking on her new prosthesis. As if she had regular legs, with no visible limp whatsoever. The girl even navigated the porch steps, taking them step over step like a normal person.

Definitely strong and independent. She never used the wheelchair anymore.

Lyn steadied herself against the car, watching in amazement. Cade had made a tremendous difference for her daughter. In light of how well Kristen was doing, Lyn wondered if perhaps she should relent on the soccer.

Inside the house, Lyn heard the door to Kristen's bedroom slam closed. Lyn wanted to talk to her girl. To explain her fears. But it'd do no good. Not when they were both so upset. Not when the memory of the car accident was still so fresh in their minds.

Instead, Lyn plopped down on a kitchen chair and sat there shaking for almost twenty minutes while she tried to sort out her feelings. Tried to think of a way to make Kristen understand she was only doing what she believed was right for both of them.

To protect Kristen. To keep her safe.

When Lyn knocked on the girl's door an hour later to announce dinner, there was a long pause.

"Go away!"

Lyn opened the door and stepped inside. Kristen lay on her bed still wearing her prosthesis, a pillow supporting her stump. She wiped her red, puffy eyes and glared.

"What do you want?"

"Honey, I hate this rift between us. We need to talk."

"No, there's nothing more to talk about." Kristen flounced around and faced the wall before jerking a second pillow to her chest.

Lyn couldn't leave things like this. Not with her precious daughter, the most important person in her life. She stepped over to the bed and would have sat down, but Kristen hunched her shoulders and jerked away.

"I hate you. Go away."

Lyn froze. The pressure of tears clogged her

throat. Though she knew it was Kristen's anger speaking, her daughter's words pierced her heart like an ice pick. Determined not to say something that would only make things worse, Lyn kept her voice smooth and calm.

"Well, I love you. I always will. Maybe someday you'll understand just how much."

Kristen didn't respond. A horrible, swelling silence followed.

Lyn turned and walked out, closing the door quietly behind her. She wrapped their untouched dinner in plastic and put it in the fridge. In her own bedroom, she stood for several minutes, gazing at Rob's picture on her bedside table, not knowing what to do. How she missed him. How she wished he were here. Every fiber of her being felt as though it were ripping apart. Her husband was gone and her daughter hated her. How had things gotten so out of control? And how could they ever get back to some level of ordinary life?

The mattress bounced as Lyn sat on the bed. A year ago, she and Rob had their entire lives together planned out. Everything was wonderful. They were so happy and in love. Now Lyn didn't have any answers. Least of all how to help Kristen. They loved each other, of that Lyn had no doubt. But they were no longer friends. And that hurt most of all.

Lyn stared at the red lights of the clock radio on the nightstand, wondering how she could heal the shattered divide between her and Kristen. Tears flooded her eyes. A lump rose in her throat, and her body shook. She covered her face with her hands and wept.

"You shouldn't be helping that woman. She's the enemy."

Cade glanced at Billie Shining Elk, one of the Shoshone tribal leaders. The two men sat facing each other inside Cade's living room. Cade couldn't wrap his mind around Billie's words. Lyn was his enemy? How ridiculous.

"I'm a doctor. This is what I do. I help people," Cade said.

"You shouldn't help her. She'll think she can run over us with the wild horses," Billie insisted.

"Her daughter is my patient. She's just a little girl."

Billie shrugged and took a sip from the tin mug he held in his leathered hand. The aroma of coffee filtered through the air. "It's the same thing. Lice have nits. They're one and the same. Helping the daughter helps the mother."

Cade stared at the Shoshone chief, his insides broiling. He couldn't explain why, but he didn't like Billie referring to Lyn as lice or Kristen as a nit. They were human beings with feelings and troubles of their own. In spite of her profession,

Cade had found Lyn to be a very thoughtful, caring woman. He liked her. A lot.

"They aren't vermin. They're good people," Cade said.

He wished the Indian chief hadn't paid an early-morning visit. The tribal members knew he was communicating with Lyn. They liked the idea of him keeping their "enemy" close so they could find out what she planned with regards to the mustangs. They didn't mind Cade spying on the ranger, but they didn't want him to provide physical therapy for her daughter.

Billie let out a derisive snort. "She's already contaminated you with her thoughts. Your job is to protect the wild horses, not help the ranger get rid of them."

"Lyn is trying to save the mustangs, too."

"Lyn? You're on a first-name basis with her?"

"Of course. I've spent quite a bit of time getting to know her. She cares about all the wildlife on the range, not just the ranchers' cattle."

And yet, a nibbling doubt filled Cade's mind. Though he'd listened to Lyn's reasoning, he also knew she'd do what she had to in order to ensure the survival of all the wildlife out on the range. And Cade couldn't blame her. Not after what he'd seen with her. If the Shoshone Tribe couldn't come up with some other options, the horses would be rounded up. Right now, Cade found himself between a rock and a hard case.

"It's not your job to help the ranger get rid of the wild horses," Billie insisted.

"I'm not doing that at all," Cade growled, feeling defensive in spite of trying to maintain his composure. "I'm a doctor. It's my duty to help Kristen Warner for as long as she needs me."

The chief waved a calloused hand in the air. "Bah! Send her somewhere else. She can go to the doctors in Reno and good riddance."

Something went cold inside of Cade. The thought of not seeing Kristen and Lyn every week for the girl's therapy sessions or when they came to his ranch to visit Lightning left him feeling hollow and empty inside. "Have you met the ranger and her little girl? They're nice people. The girl is an amputee. She lost her father in a terrible car accident a year ago and has had a rough time of it since then. They both have."

And they needed Cade. Badly. Of that he was convinced.

Billie stood and placed a gruff hand on Cade's shoulder, looking down at him with an edge of condescension. "Don't forget who you are, son. Your grandfather would want you to remember the things he taught you. Your mother threw away her heritage. She turned her back on her own people. I hope you won't do that, too."

Something hardened inside of Cade. He also stood and met the elderly chief's piercing eyes without flinching. "I remember very well. Grandfather taught me to care for all animals and people. To do what is right, no matter what. Just like my mother did when she married my father. That's why I became a medical doctor. And that's what I'm trying to do."

Billie dropped his hand away and stepped back. His creased face hardened with resolve. "And the tribal elders will do what they believe is right."

"Tell them they're worrying about nothing. Our argument isn't with a ten-year-old child," Cade said.

"No, it's with her mother." Billie spoke low.

Cade shook his head. "It's with legislation carried out by the BLM."

Billie's mouth tightened with disapproval. Cade wished the chief could know Lyn the way he did. Thank goodness the tribal leaders didn't know about Lightning. Cade doubted they'd approve of him keeping a little filly out here at Sunrise Ranch for Kristen to visit anytime she pleased. But it was more than that. The little foal's story was something special that Cade shared with Lyn and Kristen alone. He didn't want to expose that special tale to anyone else. At least not yet. And that confused Cade. He couldn't make sense of his fond feelings for the forest ranger and her little girl.

Not when Lyn was the one person in the world he should despise.

"You have nothing to worry about," Cade assured the chief. "I'm having regular discussions with Mrs. Warner, watching what she does and finding out her plans. I've provided that information to the tribe."

"Does she plan to call in the BLM for a horse roundup?"

Cade paused, not wanting to speak the truth, but unwilling to lie. "Not quite yet, but the mustangs are starving. Eventually, I believe she'll have no other choice."

The creases around Billie's eyes deepened in a scowl. "That's what I feared. We'll have to do something about it soon."

The sounds of an engine came from outside. Cade didn't need to look out the window to know the object of their discussion had just pulled into his yard with her horse trailer in tow.

Great! Cade had hoped Billie would be long gone before Lyn arrived to pick him up for their next excursion into the mountains. Though it was just past eight in the morning, Billie had arrived an hour earlier. Cade hadn't finished his chores, including feeding Lightning.

"Looks like you have another visitor." With a wave of his hand, Billie brushed the curtains aside.

When he saw Lyn, his face tensed with displeasure. He glared at Cade, his eyes filled with accusation.

"Thanks for stopping by," Cade said. He urged the chief toward the front door. It'd be best to get the man out of here as fast as possible, hopefully before he insulted Lyn.

As he jerked open the door before Lyn could knock, Cade felt as though he were riding a wild steer in a rodeo. When he got bucked off, he might get stomped into the ground.

Cade couldn't deny the values he shared with his Shoshone people. Neither could he ride the fence rail without getting hurt. Eventually, he would be forced to pick a side. He just hoped he didn't get gored in the process.

Chapter Eight

"Hi, there." Lyn greeted Cade and the older man with him. She gave them a friendly smile as she scratched Gus's neck. The dog panted blissfully. And that made Lyn happy on a day when she needed cheering up.

A lot of cheering up.

It was her birthday, and no one knew. Except her. She wasn't about to walk around telling people. Not even Kristen remembered, although Lyn couldn't fault her daughter. The girl was still too young to think about special days other than her own. In fact, Lyn wished she could forget it, too. Without Rob here to share the occasion, she didn't care. It was just an ordinary day like any other.

At least, she tried to pretend it was.

"Good morning," Cade responded.

The other gentleman glowered. Lyn recognized him from the doctor's office. The long, black hair with an eagle feather. His piercing gaze swept past her like she wasn't there. He'd been the man whose wife Maya had threatened to call if he didn't take his medication.

Billie. That was his name.

"Lyn, this is Chief Billie Shining Elk. One of the tribal elders. He was just leaving."

"Oh! You're Mr. Shining Elk. I've called your office several times. I'd like to meet with you and the other tribal elders to discuss the wild horses, if that's possible. Did you receive my letter, by chance?" Lyn asked politely.

Billie grunted and brushed past her without acknowledgment. Lyn stared after him in stunned silence.

"Thanks for stopping by," Cade called to the man.

"You think on my words," Billie said over his shoulder before hopping off the wraparound porch.

Lyn stepped to one side, trying to keep her face devoid of expression. But she understood the situation without Cade uttering a single word of explanation. She'd seen this before. The chief didn't like her because she was the forest ranger. A potential threat to the wild horses. No doubt he'd been voicing his concerns to Cade. It was that simple.

Billie placed his cowboy hat on his head and sauntered over to his rusty truck. His high cheekbones and regal bearing spoke of pride. A commanding presence she couldn't deny. She respected him for who he was and what he represented. She just wished he would extend her the same courtesy.

"Well, that was rude. Did I do something wrong?" She stood beside Cade on the front porch, staring after Billie as he started his truck and pulled out of the front yard.

"Not yet."

"He doesn't like me." She sensed it with every fiber of her being.

"He fears you."

She glanced at Cade in surprise. "He doesn't even know me."

"He's afraid of what you'll do to the wild horses."

"I don't want to do anything to the mustangs, except help them." She reached up and touched the bronze shield pinned above the front pocket of her Forest Service shirt. It gleamed in the morning sunlight. A subtle reminder of her job and some of the uncomfortable tasks she must perform, whether people liked it or not.

"Apparently the members of the Toyakoi Tribe don't like me providing physical therapy to Kristen, either," Cade said.

"I see. They don't want you treating the forest ranger's daughter."

"That's right." He slipped his hands into his pants pockets, still gazing at the billow of dust rising along the dirt road to herald Billie's passing.

Lyn stood there thinking, wondering if Cade would refuse to treat Kristen anymore. She had to know in case she had to make arrangements for another doctor. "So what do you intend to do?"

She couldn't forget the animosity fogging Billie's dark eyes—hostility toward her. Now was a moment of truth. She'd find out what Cade Baldwin was made of. If he'd refuse to serve Kristen because the tribal elders told him to, or stand his own ground.

He met her gaze without flinching. "I'll continue to treat Kristen, of course."

"Thank you." She inwardly breathed a sigh of relief, feeling a great deal of admiration for the handsome doctor. The nearest prosthetics specialist lived in Reno, a good four-hour drive away. It'd pose a hardship on Lyn to drive Kristen there every week to receive her physical therapy. Time away from work and school, not to mention the added expense for travel. Thankfully she wouldn't need to do that.

At least not yet. Cade could always change his mind.

"Let me get my hat and we'll go," Cade said.

He walked back inside the house for a few minutes. When he returned, Lyn had already led Flash outside the corral to the horse trailer. Cade helped her load the animal next to Apple. Together, they lifted the ramp in and shut the door.

"All ready?" he asked.

"Yes."

"Oh! I almost forgot something. Just one moment."

For a second time, he ran back into the house. When he returned, the screen door clapped closed behind him. He carried a brown paper bag and carefully placed it inside his saddle pack. He offered no explanation to its contents, and Lyn didn't ask.

She jutted her chin toward the narrow dirt road. "You don't have to go with me if you don't want to, Cade. I understand this might cause a conflict between you and your tribe."

"I want to go." He looked straight ahead, his jaw locked.

"I just don't want you to get into trouble with your friends."

"Actually, they want me to go with you. In fact, they're the ones who asked me to do it in the first place. They just don't want me to help Kristen."

"You mean they want you to spy, but not help me?" They'd had this conversation in the beginning, but she hadn't known then that the tribal elders had asked Cade to ride with her.

Over a month ago, she'd sent a letter asking the tribal leaders to let her meet with all of them to discuss problems and possible resolutions for the mustangs. They hadn't responded. So she'd called them. Numerous times, leaving positive messages on their voice mails. Still nothing. Their lack of response spoke loud and clear. There would be no meeting. Instead, they'd asked Cade to serve as their mole.

Cade flashed a devastating smile that made his dark eyes gleam. "I'd want to tag along even if they hadn't asked me to. I've learned a lot from you. Billie just wanted an update on the wild-horse situation. I gave it to him. End of story. I'm not spying. I'm getting an education."

Okay, she could accept that. She didn't have another choice.

Settling her cowboy hat on her head, she gave him a knowing frown. "I have nothing to hide, Cade. If you want to know something, just ask. But I also have to follow the laws and approved environmental plans."

"I know. And it's not Kristen's fault the BLM might be called in to round up some of the mustangs. Nor is it fair to stop treating her because I don't like the legislation used against the wild horses. That's what I told Billie. I still want to protect the mustangs if at all possible, but I want to be reasonable, too. I hope you'll do the same."

She nodded once. "Understood. I appreciate your candor."

"Why don't we focus on work now?"

"That sounds good to me." She climbed into the

truck, wishing there could be no trouble with the Shoshone Tribe, but knowing that was almost impossible now.

As they drove into the mountains, Lyn explained that they would be checking on a water cistern the Forest Service had installed at Wilkin's Peak the previous fall.

"I saw it when it was brand-new and filled with cool, clear water for the local wildlife," Cade said.

"Apparently it's not that way anymore."

He frowned, his body swaying easily as they drove over the rutted road. "What do you mean?"

"I've been told it's now in poor repair."

"But it's not even a year old."

"That's right."

"What do you think caused the damage?"

Her knuckles whitened as she tightened her fingers around the steering wheel. She pressed the brakes as they came to a dip in the washboard road. "Why don't we just take a look before we make any accusations?"

He gave a huffing laugh. "In other words, you think the horses are to blame."

"I didn't say that, Cade."

"But someone else did. One of your employees, maybe?"

She didn't respond. It'd do no good to confirm what he already knew. Her range assistant had given her a full report, along with a myriad of graphic photographs. But she'd wait until she saw the cistern with her own eyes and make her own deductions.

Cade shook his head. "Maybe it's not as bad as you think. At least, I hope not."

"Me, too." And she meant it. Because more trouble just added up the reasons for her to call in the BLM for a roundup. The thought of calling the BLM made her stomach churn. At first, these outings with Cade had been about the mustangs. But now, it meant something more personal to Lyn. She didn't want to hurt a kind doctor she and Kristen had both come to admire. But more important, Lyn didn't want to lose Cade's friendship.

She'd call in the BLM only as a last resort.

Something was wrong. Cade sensed it as they rode their horses across the barren hillside toward the water cistern. Lyn seemed overly subdued and quiet today. No extra chatter as she pointed out problems with the watershed or discussed the lack of vegetation in the area. Something was bothering her. And he wondered if it had to do with the Shoshone Tribe, the wild-horse problems, Kristen, or all three.

"It's hard to believe, but this area looks even worse than Barton's Canyon. Very desolate," he observed.

"Yes, it is. Without the cistern, there's no water

source here for the local wildlife. Just a barren wasteland. It's been like this for thirty years."

He waited for her to elaborate on this, but she didn't speak. Her body moved easily in the saddle, flowing with the gait of her Appaloosa mare. Gus's panting and the sounds of their horses' hooves striking the ground filled the air. A peaceful summer day.

"How's Kristen doing this week?" he asked.

"Fine. She walks like a pro, needing very little help. She refuses to use her wheelchair at home and even forgets to remove the C-Leg before she goes to bed. The prosthesis is a part of her now." She didn't look at him, but her mouth tightened.

Okay, he took that as a sign. Kristen was obviously heavy on her mind. And maybe he could help.

"She's sure made a great deal of progress in her physical therapy. I can't believe how physically strong she's gotten," he said.

"Yeah."

Yep, definitely bothering her.

"Something on your mind?" he couldn't help asking.

Her gaze glanced off his. "Why do you ask?"

"You don't seem your normal bubbly self today."

She quirked one brow, tilted her head and looked at him with amusement. "Bubbly? That's an interesting way to describe me."

Just one of the many words he would choose. *Intelligent, outgoing, compassionate* and *lovely* fit her well, too, but he doubted she wanted to hear compliments right now.

"I thought perhaps you were still upset over what happened with Kristen," he said.

That was blunt, but he couldn't think of another way to get Lyn to confide in him. Her personal life wasn't his business, but as Kristen's doctor, he thought he should know of possible troubles impacting his newest patient.

Her eyes crinkled in a frown. "What do you mean?"

He decided to be honest. "Her forging her application so she could play soccer without your permission."

Lyn's head snapped around, and she stared at him in disapproving surprise. "How did you know she'd forged her application?"

He shrugged. "It's a small town, and people talk."

She snorted and shook her head. "It's no one else's business."

"I know, but I'm her doctor and a bit concerned. For both of you."

Her shoulders tensed as she tightened her grip around the reins. "You needn't be. I'm her mother, and I'll deal with it appropriately."

"I know you will, but maybe I can help. After

what you and Kristen have been through, it can't be easy dealing with everything on your own."

"We'll make out just fine. We always have."

Another long period of silence followed. He should shut his mouth and leave this topic alone. But something pushed him onward, like a runaway team of horses. He cared about this woman and her child. He couldn't stop it now to save his life.

"Is there anything I can do to help?" he asked.

"No." And then she blurted out the words. "My own daughter hates me, Cade. Ever since the accident, she seems so sullen and distant. We used to be close, but now we just can't seem to get past what happened. The only time Kristen smiles is when we're with you and Lightning."

Wow, he hadn't expected her to open up that much. He was a medical doctor, trained to help deal with such problems. But perhaps because of his own experience with war, he felt suddenly inadequate. He should refer her to a psychologist in Reno. "Have you tried talking to her about it?"

"Yes, but she insists everything is fine. When she's not doing homework, she stares out the window, like she's waiting for something."

"Waiting for what?"

She shrugged one shoulder. "Beats me. She won't tell me a thing. It's like I'm her enemy. We're complete strangers."

"Maybe you should let her play soccer. It's better than having her just sitting around moping." He hoped she wouldn't take offense at his suggestion.

"No, this is something else. And I feel like if I can get to the bottom of it, we can both start to heal."

He paused, choosing his next words carefully. "Have you considered talking to God about it?"

A clipped sigh escaped her lips. "That's a rather personal question, don't you think?"

"Yes, you're right. I don't mean to stick my nose where it doesn't belong, but it might help."

Cade left it at that. The last thing he wanted to do was lecture this pretty woman. She was hurting, and he didn't want to add to that hardship. But they'd made headway. Lyn had confided her frustration over Kristen and was looking for resolutions, which was a start. When people started to talk about their problems, they usually discovered their own solutions. Right now, Lyn needed time to internalize their conversation. She'd come around—he hoped.

He reached for her hand and gave it a reassuring squeeze. "Don't worry. Everything's gonna be all right."

She showed a weak smile. "If only I dared believe you."

"You can believe me." And yet, he doubted his own words.

For now, he focused on the water cistern. A

round, metal container approximately thirty feet wide and sitting in the middle of a dust bowl. The carcasses of two small mammals lay inside. Rodents of some kind.

Cade noticed a major problem right off. The cistern was empty, the water all drained out around the perimeter to create a wide mud hole. A melee of hoofprints showed the recent use by unshod horses. Mustangs. Nothing but sage and rabbit brush grew within the valley, but the horses must still be coming here to drink.

Lyn stepped off her mount and handed the reins to Cade so Apple wouldn't wander off. He watched as she walked the perimeter, studying the ground before she inspected the empty cistern. Standing inside the dry container, she bent over the side to examine the base of the tank. She released a heavy sigh and shook her head.

"Why is all the water on the outside of the tank? Is there a leak?" he asked.

She placed her hands on her hips, her gaze scanning the mud. "No, but they built the cistern without a way for small animals to get out so they won't drown." She pointed at the dead mammals. "Their next mistake was they built the pipeline with PVC pipe. This line is over a mile long, but it needs to be more durable, especially around the tank. The horses dig down and knock off the pipe that actually fills the trough. That empties the tank of usable water. Then the horses mill around and cause all this mud."

He stared at the broken pipes at the base of the tank, following what she said. "What should they have built the pipe with?"

"Galvanized steel. It costs a lot more and won't keep the horses from digging down, but they won't be able to damage it with their hooves as easily."

She stepped over the edge of the tank and walked back to Apple before gathering the reins in her hands.

"What are you gonna do about it?" Cade couldn't help asking. He knew without this cistern, the wild horses would have to travel a long distance to drink. They needed water here.

She put her foot in the stirrup, gripped the saddle horn and pulled herself up. The leather creaked as she sat back. She was so graceful and light on her feet. "I'm going to try to find more money to re-build the cistern with galvanized steel and include a way for small animals to exit the tank. That'll re-quire heavy trenching machinery. I'll have to think about how that might impact reptiles and rodents and the possible damage to their burrows."

He tilted his head. "Huh?"

Turning in the saddle, she met his gaze. "This isn't an easy issue, Cade. It's quite complicated. If the horses eat the vegetation and destroy water sources, it impacts creatures as small as birds, who feed on seeds and insects. If there's no vegetation, then there are no bugs, no birds, no food for Golden Eagles, snakes and other carnivores. You understand the food chain, right? The damage done by wild horses impacts all creatures living within this area. I know snakes aren't generally considered as pretty as a wild horse, but they're just as important."

"I agree, but I admit I never contemplated that."

"Most people don't, but it's my job to think about it and take positive action to protect them all."

"Oh."

No, he'd never given these other animals a single thought. Raptors, rodents and reptiles weren't on his list of favorites, but he knew they were necessary, too. Even he realized when nature got out of balance, bad things happened. And he suspected that was what was happening with too many wild horses on the range.

Lyn clicked her heels lightly against Apple's sides, and the horse stepped forward. Cade followed as Lyn voiced a mental list of considerations.

"There'll also be displacement of the wildlife during construction of the new cistern. I'll have to think of a way to provide another water source during that period of time. And maybe we'll need to install a cattle guard at the north end of Dixon Canyon."

"A cattle guard?"

"Yeah, I don't want cows coming in here to graze for a few years. There aren't a lot grazing here now, but they might still come in for water and prevent the vegetation from recovering. All we can do is try."

Such a complicated subject. Cade never knew. And yet, he couldn't fault Lyn for trying to help the mustangs and other wildlife living out here.

As they rode back to the Forest Service truck, Cade found himself deep in thought. Troubled. Wondering how to weigh his preconceived notions with what he'd learned on these outings with Lyn and what the tribal elders wanted. Things he never knew or considered before. Issues he'd need to report to the tribal leaders at their next meeting on Monday night. And he doubted they'd like his findings. As much as he wanted the mustangs left alone in their natural habitat, he wouldn't lie. Not when it meant the deterioration of other wildlife.

Cade thought about asking Lyn to accompany him and make a presentation to the tribe, but decided against that. The tribe didn't want her there. They figured they knew everything already. The BLM always consulted with the tribe before rounding up wild horses, and the meetings were tense, loud and angry. He didn't want to subject Lyn to that kind of animosity. And yet, he knew it was her job, so he doubted she would shy away if he asked her to do it. Why was he trying to shield her, then? Why did he feel so protective of her and Kristen?

None of his feelings made sense. He just didn't understand himself anymore.

Lyn lifted the saddle from Apple's back and set it on a sliding rack in the horse trailer. Removing her hat, she wiped her brow. Because it was her birthday, she missed Rob more than usual. Being with Cade lessened her sadness.

She turned, preparing to climb into the cab and drive them to Sunrise Ranch, but hesitated. Cade stood before her, holding the brown paper bag he'd retrieved from his house earlier. He smiled wide, showing perfect, white teeth. A glint of mischief shimmered in his eyes.

"Before we go home, I have something special I want to give you," he said.

Her mouth went dry. Standing frozen on the ground, she watched as he reached inside the bag and removed an oblong, plastic container with a red lid. He tossed the sack aside, and the plastic lid made a sucking sound as he popped it off. Two huge cupcakes decorated with fluffy, pink icing sat inside. Reaching into his pocket, he pulled out a small lighter. After he poked a slim candle into the top of one cupcake, he lit the short wick and broke into a baritone rendition of "Happy Birthday."

Lyn couldn't move. She felt glued in place. Like the whole world stood still.

He lifted the cupcake toward her, moving slow so the flickering flame wouldn't go out. "Make a wish and blow out the candle, Ranger."

His gaze locked with hers, his eyes seeing beyond the protective wall she'd erected around her heart. Tears burned the backs of her eyes, but she didn't let them fall. Cade had no idea what he'd done. How hard it was for her to accept his gift. Or what it meant to her.

As if sensing her discomposure, he stepped closer, his smile fading to a look of concern. "You okay, Lyn?"

She nodded and glanced at the cupcake, her chin quivering. Rob had always brought her a cupcake on her birthdays, although much smaller, along with a wrapped present. Usually a piece of jewelry she wore on special occasions or on Sundays for church.

"I hope you like white cake," he said. "I didn't make these myself, though. I bought them from the bakery in town." He was smiling again, but not quite as wide. As if he was nervous she wouldn't like his offering.

"Wh-white is fine. My favorite."

His smile widened with pleasure. "Good. Happy birthday. Now make a wish."

"How…how did you know it was my birthday?"

When no one else in the world knew, he'd found out somehow. That was a disconcerting thought.

"Remember, I have Kristen's and your medical records at my office."

Ah. She hadn't thought about that. But she didn't want him for her doctor. He was great with Kristen, but letting him treat her seemed a bit too personal. Revealing her physical and mental concerns to this man made her feel odd. After all, he was just interested in saving the wild horses.

And yet, he'd become so much more to her.

"But why would you do this for me?" Most men weren't so considerate.

He shrugged. "I know you and Kristen are alone, just like me. I know what it's like to celebrate holidays on your own, and it's not fun. I didn't want that for you."

His thoughtfulness touched her like nothing else could. She liked him the way a woman liked a man she hoped might ask her out on a date. And that didn't seem right, for too many reasons to count. Rob had been gone barely a year. It was too soon to think of dating someone else. Wasn't it? Kristen would never accept another man to replace her father anyway.

Neither would Lyn.

Ignoring her thoughts, she made a quick wish and blew out the candle, feeling exposed. And guilty. Because her wish had been for herself, and not Kristen. Lyn wasn't used to putting herself above her daughter. Not for a long, long time.

"Good one." Cade laughed, melting her frustration with his warm gaze.

She didn't move as he plucked the smoking candle from the frosting, then handed the cupcake to her. She held the confection dumbly in her hand. Cade didn't wait, but picked up his own cake and bit into it. A splotch of pink frosting stuck to the corner of his mouth. She watched as he licked it away, feeling warm and fuzzy inside. Though she never showed it, she felt bone weary and tired of thinking she'd never be happy again. Tired of dealing with Kristen's sullenness. Tired of everything. But Cade had eased that somehow. With a smile and a cupcake.

Her gaze swung upward, and she regarded him openly. The terrain seemed to swim around her in bouncing waves. And for the first time that day, she laughed out loud.

"Ah, there you are." He nudged her hand gently with his elbow, urging her to take a bite of cake.

She did, no longer fighting him. Instead, she enjoyed the sweet taste of buttercream icing on her tongue and tried to ignore the odd fluttering in her chest, wondering what was wrong with her.

It took only moments to wolf down their cakes, but they were moments of wonder and relief for Lyn. It was her birthday, and someone had remembered to celebrate her life. That meant a lot. She'd never forget Cade's kindness.

"Thank you. This was very nice of you," she said.

"Did Kristen make you something special?"

Lyn shook her head. "No, she didn't remember."

"I should have reminded her."

Red heat enveloped her. "That's not your job."

"But I knew and didn't tell her."

"This was enough. Thank you."

He picked up the paper bag and stowed the plastic container inside. "You're very welcome, Mrs. Warner."

"I'm not a missus anymore." The moment she said the words, she regretted them. It made her feel disloyal to Rob and all the years ahead that she wouldn't get to share her life with him. She wasn't ready to move on and let him go.

At least, not yet.

"Yes, I know…Lyn," Cade corrected.

Without waiting for her reaction, he tossed a remnant of his cupcake to Gus, then walked around to his side of the truck. The dog chomped down on the treat and trotted after his master.

Taking a deep breath, Lyn released it and gained her composure. She hadn't planned it, but she counted Cade as a good friend. Without her telling him anything, he seemed to know her so well. And yet, he knew nothing about her. Not really.

They weren't supposed to grow closer together. She wasn't supposed to confide in him or share her concerns about Kristen. But she had.

Confused by their growing relationship, Lyn climbed inside the truck, started the ignition and drove them back to town.

Chapter Nine

Kristen wouldn't like this. Neither did Lyn. Being late picking her daughter up from physical therapy went against Lyn's grain. As usual, work had interrupted her day. After dropping Kristen off, she'd raced back to the office to deal with another problem. Now Lyn tapped on the brake, slowing the car as she drove through town. A sheen of dampness wet her brow. She wiped it away and flipped on the air conditioner, too distracted to enjoy the beautiful afternoon. Taking a deep inhale, she tried to settle her nerves. Too much to do. Too many distractions.

Thinking of the packs of purple pansies and yellow marigolds she had waiting at home, Lyn smiled. After picking Kristen up from therapy, she planned to take her daughter to the diner for a cheeseburger and fries before going home to work in their flower garden. Lyn's fingers almost itched to dig in the soil. No ringing phones. No demands. Just her and Kristen, spending quality time together.

Turning the corner, Lyn pulled over and parked in front of the doctor's office. The bell above the door tinkled as she walked inside the reception room. Maya sat behind the long counter and greeted her with a smile.

"Hi, Ms. Warner. They're out back." Maya jutted her chin toward the far door.

Lyn yanked her gaze in that direction. She'd expected her daughter to be working inside the therapy gait room Cade had set up. "What are they doing outside?"

Maya shrugged. "A new type of physical therapy Dr. Baldwin's trying out."

Hmm. That seemed odd.

Lyn pressed against the push plate on the back door and stepped out into the sunshine. The vacant lot behind the clinic stood empty, the dirt cleared of weeds. Cade's truck and horse trailer sat parked nearby. Lyn couldn't see her daughter, but she could hear her lilting voice mingled with the deep timbre of Cade's laugh.

And another man's voice Lyn didn't recognize.

Lyn stepped around the truck, a smile on her face. She froze in midstep. Her smile dropped like stone, and she clenched her hands.

Kristen sat astride Magpie, the old mare Cade kept out at his ranch. He stood nearby, but the girl held the reins, bouncing gently in the saddle as the horse trotted in a wide, arching circle. The clop of horse hooves filled Lyn's ears in pounding waves.

Another man Lyn didn't recognize rode beside the child on Flash. Both men shouted encouragement to the girl. They were all having a great time, and they seemed oblivious to the potential dangers.

Paralyzing fear held Lyn in an icy grip. For one horrific moment, she envisioned the car crash. Kristen screaming. And Rob's lifeless body bleeding and broken, like a rag doll.

"Wh-what are you doing?" Lyn's voice throbbed with emotion, her voice a weak whisper.

"Mom! Look at me." Kristen waved.

"Hi, Lyn." Cade reached up and gripped the horse's halter, pulling the mare to a stop.

A touch of vertigo caused Lyn to reach out and steady herself against the truck. She shook her head, fighting it off. Trying to remain calm. Trying to keep her cool. But one question pounded her brain.

Why? Why had Cade put her daughter at risk?

Bracing his hands beneath the girl's arms, Cade lifted Kristen off the mare and set her on her feet. He paused long enough for the child to set her weight and gain her balance.

Kristen laughed, breathless with happiness. Unaware of her mother's fears.

Kristen patted the animal's neck, praising the

horse. "You're such a good girl, Magpie. Thanks for letting me ride you."

The other man loped Flash over to join them. His lean body moved gracefully with the gait of the horse. He pulled to a quick stop before he lifted one leg over the saddle and jumped to the ground. He was obviously a skilled horseman.

"Wh-what are you doing?" Lyn was finally able to get the words out loud enough for the group to hear. Her gaze shifted to her daughter, but her words were for Cade.

"I was riding, Mom," Kristen said. "Did you see me? Oh, it's been so much fun. I never thought I'd ever get to ride, but Cade says I can do anything I set my mind to."

"Dr. Baldwin," Lyn corrected.

"Yeah, and he says nothing should hold me back. I'm only as handicapped as I let myself be. I was riding all by myself. Isn't that great?"

"Yeah, just great." Lyn barely heard her daughter's words. Her mind whirled. First Kristen was injured playing soccer, and now this. Her alarm gave way to absolute fury—at Cade. She took several settling breaths, trying to regain her composure. Trying not to lose control.

Instead she hugged Kristen tight, utterly relieved that her daughter was okay. No harm done. Kristen was safe. At least for now.

"Mom, you're squashing my eye." The girl pushed her away.

Lyn stepped back, her hands trembling. "I'm... I'm glad you've had a good therapy session. Now why don't you go inside and see if Maya has a lollipop for you. I saw some sitting on her counter. I need to speak with Dr. Baldwin alone for a few minutes." Her voice sounded wooden as she glanced at Cade.

He met her stare, matching the challenge she put into her eyes. Surely he knew what he'd done. Didn't he? He knew she didn't condone taking chances with Kristen, yet he'd done it anyway. And he'd had no right. No right at all.

"Okay." Oblivious to the silent battle waging around her, the girl turned and gripped Cade's hand. "Thanks again for letting me ride Magpie, Dr. Baldwin. I like this kind of physical therapy better than exercising on a floor mat. I can't wait until Lightning's old enough for me to ride."

Lyn blinked, her heart aching. Her daughter freely showed Cade the affection she craved from her child. Something Lyn coveted like the air she breathed. But because she loved her daughter unconditionally, Lyn had to fight off waves of resentment. Ugly emotions she refused to let take hold of her soul. How she wished Kristen loved her the way she used to.

Cade's gaze slid from Lyn's face to the girl's,

and he patted Kristen's cheek. "You're welcome, sweetheart. But it'll be a couple of years before Lightning can be ridden. Be sure to do your exercises at home anyway. You're making great headway, but we want to keep strengthening your legs."

"I will. I promise." Kristen turned toward the stranger and waved. "See you next time, Dal."

Dal. He must be a friend of Cade's. But Lyn didn't care. She had other pressing matters on her mind right now. Like what she should say to Cade.

Both men smiled as the girl walked to the door with barely a limp. If not for the prosthesis showing below the cuffed hem of her knee-length shorts, they couldn't even tell the girl was an amputee. Cade's techniques had been working, but he'd gone too far this time. And Lyn couldn't let it continue.

The moment the door whooshed closed behind Kristen, Lyn whirled on Cade. "What do you think you're doing?"

He blinked in surprise, then gestured toward the man named Dal. "Lyn, I'd like you to meet my good friend Dallin Savatch. We served in the war together. Dal's an expert rider."

Dal was a tall, handsome man with a square-jawed face, generous lips and sand-colored hair cut high and tight like a U.S. marine. He had a lean runner's body with a wide chest and shoulders and long, muscular legs that went on forever.

"Nice to meet you." Her clipped words were

spoken fast and by rote. No emotion and no interest whatsoever.

Lyn ignored the hand Dal extended and barely spared the smiling man a glance before she repeated her question to Cade. She didn't mean to be rude, but she was highly upset. This couldn't happen again. She had to make sure.

Cade jabbed his fingers through his short hair. "Look, Lyn, I know you're angry right now. But I was beside Kristen the entire time she was riding. Her self-esteem has taken a giant turn for the better. She's had a great time today. Riding is good for her."

"No." She shook her head, refusing to hear what he said. Refusing to accept this course of therapy.

"Yes, it is," he insisted. "As she hugs the sides of the horse with her legs, it strengthens her thigh and calf muscles. I've worked with her on her posture, which will strengthen her abdomen and back."

"I don't care, Cade. Give her some different exercises to strengthen her muscles. Something that keeps her safely on the ground."

He arched a brow. "You mean something in your control?"

She skewered him with her glare. "Yes!"

His eyes darkened like ripe, black olives. A long, horrible silence followed as they stared at each other, now standing toe-to-toe. Lyn didn't know how they'd gotten so close. She couldn't remember stepping over to the doctor. Or perhaps he'd moved toward her. So close, she could see a small, white scar along the edge of his left eyebrow.

"Do you realize what you're saying?" he asked. His voice was whisper-soft and filled with disapproval.

"It's my job to protect her."

His jaw hardened. "Protect her, yes. But don't stifle her, Lyn. You're holding on too tight. Let her live. Let her learn and grow and be her own person. That's the only way she'll ever be able to lead a normal, happy life."

"I can't take the risk."

"Yes, you can."

"And what if she gets hurt again?" The thought made her stomach clench.

"Then we'll deal with it. We'll be here for her. Always."

She sucked in a harsh breath. "You'll be here? You're just her doctor, Cade. You're not her father. If Kristen gets injured, it won't impact your life whatsoever. You'll go on like nothing ever happened while I deal with the fallout. You had no right to do this. I'm her mother." Oh, it was so tempting to yell and screech at him. But she didn't. Not at all.

But inside she was screaming.

His mouth tightened perceptibly. "I'm sorry, but I care about Kristen, more than I can say. I care about you, too. If you continue down this path, you're going to lose your daughter for good one day. And I'm not talking about death or injury." His voice sounded so deadly calm. Which made it even more frightening.

Lyn iced over, her knees wobbling so hard she could barely stand. She couldn't accept what he said. Outside of normal compassion, he couldn't possibly care for them. They weren't married. They weren't a family.

They weren't anything.

Cade couldn't believe this situation. How had things gotten so out of hand? Obviously, he'd lost Lyn's trust, but he hadn't intended to. Now he had to make things right. This was a moment of truth between them. Lyn could make a lot of trouble for him. A malpractice suit might destroy his medical career, or at least his reputation. Would Lyn do something so horrible?

"Do you want to sue me?" he asked cautiously.

Dismayed surprise filled her eyes. "Of course not. I just want to know my daughter is safe when I drop her off at your office."

"I'd never let anything bad happen to Kristen. I thought you knew that. I thought we were friends. Good friends."

She chewed her bottom lip, her eyes wide with

alarm. She looked suspicious and hunted. "I thought so, too, but now I'm not so sure."

"Lyn, you can trust me to do what's right for Kristen. I want to show you something." He pivoted toward Dal.

Lyn looked at the other man and blinked, as though she'd forgotten he was here, listening to this entire tirade. For a few minutes, Cade had forgotten his friend, too.

"Dal, would you mind showing Lyn your legs?" Cade asked.

Lyn's gaze lowered to Dal's limbs. Cade could see the question in her honey-brown eyes. Nothing appeared out of the ordinary. Just a pair of long legs sheathed in faded denims and worn cowboy boots.

Dal didn't smile as he bent over and rolled up his pant legs. Lyn stared at one strong, muscular calf dusted with dark hair. Dal's left leg was a C-Leg prosthesis. Almost identical to the one Kristen wore, except bigger and longer to accommodate his greater height and weight.

Understanding filled Lyn's eyes. Dal was an amputee. Just like Kristen.

"Dal saved my life in Afghanistan," Cade said. "He lost his leg above the knee in the process, but he didn't lose his will to live. He's one of the fastest men in the world. A few years ago, he won the 100-meter dash and a few other races in the Paralympics."

Lyn's gaze darted up to Dal's face. The man stood there, tall and proud. A U.S. marine who'd given so much for his country. Cade owed everything to this good man, and they loved each other like brothers. The best of friends.

"I'm sorry for all that you've lost," Lyn said.

Dal inclined his head. "Thank you, ma'am."

Lyn faced Cade again, her expression hardening. And he knew nothing had changed between them. Not for her and Kristen.

"I'm sorry, Cade, but I'll be taking Kristen into Reno to a therapist from now on. We won't be coming to you anymore."

Cade swallowed hard, his stomach churning. "Don't do that, Lyn. We can work this out. If you feel that strongly about it, I won't put Kristen on a horse again. Just don't take her away."

He was almost begging. And he wondered why it was so important that they stay with him. He didn't understand, but he knew deep inside that if he lost them, he'd be losing something he could never replace.

"My mind's made up. I need to be able to trust the doctors I take my child to," she said.

"You can trust me. I'm sorry for today. So sorry. I thought if I showed you how well she could do on a horse, you'd change your mind about letting her ride. It won't happen again. I promise." If only she'd believe him. He had nothing but Kristen's best interests at heart. He didn't want them to go.

Lyn gestured toward the horses. "It's too great a risk."

"I made a medical decision, Lyn. I thought riding was the best therapy for her. Right now, she feels good. Like she can do anything."

"Yes, and she can't. You've filled her head with nonsense. Impossible goals she can never reach. Your encouragement will do nothing but bring her heartache and disappointment."

His mouth dropped open in amazement. "That's phooey. Are you listening to yourself? You're Kristen's mom, and yet you know nothing about her. Did you know her greatest dream is to have her own horse and compete in the rodeo like her dad? She wants to barrel race."

"Yes, I've known she wanted a horse for a very long time, but the rodeo is impossible. Maybe not now, but sometime in the future she'll get bucked off. She'll get hurt again. I can't let that happen. Not ever."

"You can't lock her up in her room, Lyn."

"My mind is made up." Lyn shot past him, marching toward the clinic. Her spine was straight and unyielding, her shoulders stiff with determination.

Cade stared after her, feeling lost and aggravated. If only he could make Lyn see how wrong she was. He'd never met a more maddening woman in all his life.

Exasperating and beautiful.

As the door whisked closed behind her, he felt completely lost and all alone. The thought of not treating Kristen or seeing Lyn again left him feeling…what?

Empty and bereft.

"Don't you think it's time you told her the truth?" Dal spoke beside him, an understanding smile curving his full lips.

Cade glanced at his good friend, his mind fogged by annoyance. "What do you mean?"

"You're in love with her."

"And you've had too much sun," Cade returned.

He reached down and gathered up the reins before leading Magpie over to the trailer. He'd brought the horses into town especially for Kristen's therapy today. He'd never gone to this much trouble for any of his other patients. Of course, Kristen was special. His only amputee. And Cade loved helping her. Loved watching the light of understanding flare within her eyes as she succeeded with the small tasks he gave her.

He liked being with Lyn, too. Riding through the mountains as they discussed horses and studied the mustangs and how to help them and the other wildlife. He couldn't deny he liked her. But love?

"How long have we known each other?" Dal asked.

Cade unhitched the saddle from Flash's back, not liking the direction this conversation was taking. "Almost fourteen years."

"Closer to sixteen. And I know you pretty well." Dal grunted as he brushed Cade aside and lifted the saddle to carry over to the trailer, then set it down on its rack.

"So?"

"So, you're in love with that woman and her little girl. You might as well admit it. Don't worry, I won't tell anyone your secret."

Cade pressed a hand against the truck and gave Dal his best glare. "I'm not admitting anything. You know she's the forest ranger. We have nothing in common."

Dal snorted and brushed dust off his hands. "Not from what I've seen and heard. You both love the wild horses, you told me that yourself. You said she's a good rider. Knows how to handle herself real well. In fact, since I arrived in town yesterday afternoon, you've talked of nothing but her. And she has a little girl who needs you very much. They both do."

"Hogwash. She doesn't even know if she believes in God."

"So, convince her she's wrong."

Cade didn't answer as he turned his back and led Magpie toward the trailer. The horse's hooves thumped against the ramp as she went inside with little enticement.

Cade didn't know what to make of Dal's comments. True, he'd never felt this way about a woman before, but it couldn't be love. He respected Lyn Warner, but that was all. He wanted to help her and Kristen. Nothing more. Though they'd shared some extraordinary times together, they barely knew each other. Not really. And trying to convince her she was wrong about God in her present state of mind would be like moving a mountain one shovelful at a time.

Besides, he'd long ago given up on mushy stuff. Between the war in Afghanistan and then medical school, he'd never had much time for romance.

But what about now?

No! Definitely not with a woman like Lyn. She was too high-strung, controlling and infuriating. She was also educated, intelligent and lovely.

But love? No sirree. That wasn't an option. Not for him.

"Why don't you ask her out?" Dal suggested, as if reading Cade's mind.

"I can't. You know that."

"Why not?"

"For one thing, I don't date the mothers of my patients. For another thing, the tribal leaders would never approve."

Dal chuckled. "Your mother never cared what the tribe thought. Not when it came to your father. Besides, Kristen's no longer your patient, so her mom's now available. And you're a grown man. You don't need permission from the Shoshone chiefs to date anyone."

Dal was right, but it wasn't quite that simple. Cade didn't want trouble. It'd taken a long time to recover from his experiences at war. He still had terrible flashbacks that left him shaking. He wanted no complications to stir up his life again. And Lyn Warner was a pretty hurdle who would do nothing but confuse his life.

"How do you do it?" Cade asked Dal.

"Do what?"

"Cope with civilian life."

Dal didn't pretend to not understand. "Who said I've coped, brother?"

They both knew the horrors of war and post-traumatic stress disorder. In fact, they'd helped each other get through it all. If you could ever recover from such a thing.

"If anyone's got a right to be stressed out by life, it's you," Cade continued.

Dal flashed that good-natured grin of his and

clapped Cade on the back. "One thing's for certain. We've both earned the right to some happiness in life. And like it or not, that woman you just ticked off makes you happy. I could see that in the way you lit up the moment she arrived."

Cade snorted. "Look who's talking. You never date, either. Why aren't you married and settled down?"

Dal glanced at his legs. "You know why. I've had one fiancée dump me already because of my leg. I'm not about to try for a second. I don't enjoy rejection that much."

"Michelle isn't the only woman in the world. There are others who aren't quite as shallow."

Dal shook his head. "We're not talking about me right now. Lyn doesn't know it yet, but I can see she feels the same about you. You've just got to convince yourself and then her that you should be together."

The man turned away, heading toward the cab of the truck. No doubt he'd want to drive on their way home to Sunrise Ranch. Dal didn't let anything get in his way. At least, not anymore.

But Dal also didn't date. Didn't become involved. A hypocrite who deserved the love of a good woman as much as Cade did.

As he closed the tailgate then sat inside the truck, Cade ignored Dal's knowing grin. But Cade couldn't help wondering why he'd decided

Lyn Warner wasn't an option for him. Maybe, just maybe, he should change his mind about that.

Then again, maybe not.

"You won't be seeing Dr. Baldwin anymore." Lyn rolled the car window up as she drove home, hoping Kristen understood her decision and didn't fight her on it.

Tremors tingled over her hands, and she tightened her fingers around the steering wheel.

"Why not?" The girl looked at her, brushing strands of long, blond hair back from her sun-kissed face. No doubt she'd have some new freckles across her nose after spending the better part of the afternoon outside.

Lyn took a deep breath, feeling exhausted by today's events. "I just think it's the right move for us to make. Dr. Baldwin's a small-town doctor, honey. I want to ensure you receive the best care possible."

"But Dr. Baldwin is the best care."

"I don't think so, hon. I think we can do better."

"You just don't want me to ride horses again," Kristen accused.

Was Lyn that transparent? And why deny it? Kristen had always been so astute. It'd do no good to lie. "That's partly true. I just want you safe. I think you need another doctor from Reno."

"No!" Kristen exploded. "Dr. Baldwin's not small-town. He cares about me. More than you do. He wants me to succeed. He wants me to try new things. To prove to myself that I can do it."

Lyn jerked. She'd expected a blowup, but not quite this volatile.

"One day, you'll understand." Lyn spoke in an unruffled, insistent tone. "When you're grown-up, you can decide what you want to do. Until then, I have to make the decisions for us."

How she wished Rob was here to bring them both an element of peace. He'd always provided a leavening of calm in their home. But that was impossible now.

The girl huffed and flounced around to stare out her window again. Or rather, glare. Lyn almost flinched at the venom she saw in Kristen's eyes. Hatred and resentment—for her mother.

They drove in silence for several heart-pounding moments. Then Kristen spoke softly, and Lyn heard the shattered tears in her voice.

"Why didn't you let me die with Daddy?"

"What?" Lyn had heard the question clear enough, but it took a few moments for her to absorb the impact.

Kristen flounced around to look at her mother. A large teardrop raced down her cheek and plopped onto her lap. "I wish I'd died with Dad. You won't let me live, so why'd you bother saving me?"

Memories rushed through Lyn's mind. The crush of metal and glass. The car upside down. Rob's broken body lying battered and unmoving beside her. His empty eyes staring wide as she fought to pull Kristen from the burning vehicle.

The horror of losing her husband overshadowed every other emotion. She had to get Kristen free. Adrenaline had pumped through her body, giving her the strength to push past the crunched metal as she pulled her daughter to safety. Even then, Kristen had still lost her leg while Lyn had survived the accident with nothing more than a few scratches.

"Because I love you so much." Lyn spoke the words around a breathless hitch. She fought off the sobs that clogged her throat. She had to be strong. For Kristen. For Rob. Because that's what he would want her to do. To keep their daughter safe.

"Then why won't you let me do things, Mom? If you love me, let me try. I'm not an invalid. Dr. Baldwin said so." The plaintive request was whispered in a begging voice.

Lyn didn't reply, but she knew the answer. She couldn't let go. Not of her little girl. Not when she felt so responsible for what happened that night. No matter what Cade told them.

Lyn couldn't overcome her fear.

They didn't speak the rest of the way home. When they arrived, Kristen hurried inside the house and slammed the door in Lyn's face. Lyn stood on the welcome mat for several seconds, feeling like an outsider in her own home. Feeling as though she didn't belong. Not anywhere.

She forced herself not to react. Not to feel wounded and angry. But it was impossible. She'd hurt Kristen that day. This was the least Lyn deserved. She couldn't deny Cade's therapy had helped. A lot. Kristen walked and ran almost as well as a normal kid now.

Because of Cade. And Lyn had hurt him. A kind man she couldn't help feeling close to. A man who made her laugh and feel alive again for the first time in a long time.

What if he was right? What if she was being overprotective, stifling Kristen and holding her back? The truth kicked Lyn hard in the chops. But how could she let go when she had no other lifeline to hold on to and no one but herself to trust?

She reached out and turned the doorknob. Inside, everything was quiet, except the tick of the grandfather clock perched against the wall like a disapproving giant. The house smelled of pine cleaner from the floors she'd mopped the evening before. Clean and sterile. Just like her life.

Lyn set her purse and keys on the kitchen table and slipped off her shoes. She padded down the hallway to the back of the house, wanting time alone. Maybe later, she'd be able to entice Kristen to go outside and plant flowers with her.

Maybe not.

Inside the bathroom, Lyn stared at herself in the mirror. Though she looked the same, she barely recognized herself. The past year had taken its toll, inside and out. Faint circles beneath her eyes indicated a myriad of sleepless nights. Twin worry lines had formed on her forehead, just between her brows. Not something anyone else would notice, but still new to her. The nagging fear inside never let up. Fear that she could lose everything that meant anything to her at any moment. And the tighter she held on, the more she strangled the joy out of her life.

The more she strangled Kristen.

Cade's words about prayer came back to haunt her. At one time, she'd shared a loving relationship with the Lord and trusted Him to nurture and care for her family. She'd tried to live the best life possible and turn the rest over to Him. Free and happy.

Now she didn't trust anyone, least of all God. But living without trust had turned her into a haggard, frightened woman. A person who no longer believed in anything benevolent or lovely. And it had destroyed her relationship with Kristen.

It was also destroying Lyn's soul.

With a quick twist of her wrist, she flipped on the cold water and splashed her face. Reaching for a fresh towel, she pressed the terry cloth against her cheeks and breathed deeply of the fragrant smell of fabric softener. It helped remind her that life could be normal and mundane. That this trouble between her and Kristen would pass. Eventually.

Or would it?

Not if Lyn didn't change something. And fast.

Chapter Ten

The following week, Lyn drove Kristen into Reno for physical therapy with Dr. Fletcher. Not a fun experience. Kristen didn't speak the entire trip, didn't exert herself during her exercises, and didn't eat a single bite of pizza at lunch. The jaunty hop in her stride disappeared, and the limp returned. She wasn't even trying.

When they got home late that afternoon, Kristen refused Lyn's request that she help plant flowers in their yard and hobbled inside the house, slamming the door behind her. Later, she stared out the picture window. Watching the road for someone who wasn't there.

Determined to stay busy, Lyn changed her clothes, jerked on her canvas gloves and knelt on a foam pad in the front flowerbed. She plucked weeds and turned the rich dark soil with a hand shovel. Now and then, she glanced up to see Kristen's profile as she sat at the kitchen table. Her mouth was tight, her eyes fixed in a harsh glare.

Hating her mom.

Lyn blinked away tears of frustration and reached for another yellow marigold, popped it out of its black plastic cup and shoved it into the small hole she'd dug. Pressing tight, she packed dirt around the roots, angry at herself. Feeling guilty for taking Cade away from Kristen. Still frustrated and drained by her angry encounter with him a week earlier. She'd done the right thing, hadn't she?

Kristen missed the kind doctor. So did Lyn.

A lot.

The sound of an engine came from behind, and Lyn glanced over her shoulder. A blue truck pulled up in front of her house.

Dallin Savatch, Cade's friend, hopped out of the vehicle. Dressed in blue jeans, boots and a black T-shirt, he strode up the sidewalk toward her. Confident. Strong. Showing not a single hint that he was an amputee.

Lyn stood, brushing dirt off her work shirt. Her mind filled with a multitude of questions as she wondered what he was doing here.

"Howdy, ma'am." He flashed a smile, his hazel eyes showing no animosity.

"Hello, Mr. Savatch."

He sucked in a quick breath. "Tell you what. You can call me Dal if I can call you Lyn."

She hesitated. Being on a first-name basis with him would open doors to familiarity and bring her closer to Cade. She wasn't sure that's what she wanted, but she sure didn't like the sick feeling she'd carried inside her heart ever since her fight with the handsome doctor.

"All right...Dal."

He reached out a hand to brace against the porch railing. The gesture seemed quite casual, but Lyn recognized it as a subtle way to ease the weight on his amputated leg.

"What can I do for you?" she asked.

"Actually, it's what I can do for you."

"I don't understand."

"I know you're hurting, Lyn. Cade's told me a bit about you and Kristen. But I think it's a mistake to keep your daughter from working with Cade."

"Did he send you here?"

"No, no. I came on my own. He cares a great deal and can help Kristen."

"On his terms. I'm Kristen's mother and know what's best for her. Cade needs to respect that. He doesn't understand what we've been through or how much we've lost."

"I agree he needs to respect your decisions, but he does understand. He's been through the trauma of war. Even if I could bring myself to do so, I can't begin to tell you how bad it was over there for all of us, but especially for him."

"What do you mean?"

He shrugged one broad shoulder. "I think I better let him tell you about it when he feels the time is right."

She inwardly cringed, her imagination filling in the blanks. What was Dal talking about? Cade had been to war. Maybe even killed other men. No doubt, he'd been shot at. Lyn could understand all of that. But she got the impression that Dal was hinting at something even worse, and she couldn't visualize what that might be.

"I think you need to trust him," Dal said.

"You do, huh?" She wanted to. She really did. As much as she wanted to trust God again.

"Yeah. Give him one more chance. I promise I won't let him put Kristen on another horse, unless we can convince you otherwise."

"Well, you can't."

He nodded. "Understood. But let him work with her again. Please."

Why was this so important to Dal?

"What does it matter if Cade is Kristen's doctor?"

"He saved my life," Dal said.

She paused. "I thought you saved him."

"I did. But afterward, when I was in the hospital, it was bad. The pain and knowing I might never walk again. I couldn't get over it. Then, when I

came home, my fiancée broke off our engagement.
What woman would want half a man like me? I
thought my life was over. I wanted to die."

Her heart collapsed around his words. Was that
how Kristen felt? Like no one wanted her? Like
she didn't want to live anymore?

"I…I wanted to quit," Dal continued. "But Cade
wouldn't let me. He forced me to keep fighting. To
survive. To find joy in living again. And to have
hope."

Hope. Something Lyn had buried along with her
husband.

"But why is it so important that Cade keep working with Kristen?" She had to know. Had to understand.

He sucked in his breath. "Because being with
you and your little girl makes Cade happy. I can
see it in the way he lights up when you're around.
And I could be wrong, but I think you feel the same
about him."

Yes. No. She couldn't. Could she?

Surely Dal was imagining things. He'd only seen
her with Cade once, and they'd had a giant fight at
the time. And yet, deep in her heart of hearts, Lyn
knew he spoke the truth. She wanted to see Cade
again. To spend time riding through the mountains
with him. To take her daughter back to his office
for therapy. To play with Lightning out at Sunrise

Ranch and see him and Kristen laugh together. Being with Cade brought Lyn such peace. The first she'd known since before Rob died.

"Will you at least reconsider? As a favor to me?" Dal asked.

She nodded, against her better judgment. Against her common sense. "Yes, I'll think about it."

He released a tight breath. "Good. Thank you."

He swiveled away from her, returning to his truck. She stood there watching as he drove away. The urge to go inside and tell Kristen she was returning to Dr. Baldwin pushed her toward the front porch, but she paused. Instead, she went to the backyard where she found a sheltered spot among the trees where no one could see her. Sunlight filtered through the thick branches as the cool shadows gathered around her. She knelt down on the soft carpet of green grass. Birdsong comforted her as she rested her hands in her lap. She bowed her head, closed her eyes and prayed. Pouring her heart and soul out to God. Telling Him all her troubles and fears. Seeking guidance for the first time in a long time. Wanting to believe that the Lord was there and really cared about her and Kristen.

When she finished, Lyn stood and flexed her stiff legs and arms. Her doubts weren't completely gone, but she felt reconciled with the Lord. It wasn't everything, but it was a beginning. It was time. To take Kristen back to church. To have family prayers and discussions about the Lord.

To renew their faith.

The next day, Lyn's fledgling convictions faced yet another trial. Because of an all-day meeting at the supervisor's office, she was late picking Kristen up from school. When she arrived out front, the girl was nowhere to be seen. The swings on the blacktop sat empty, rocking gently in the breeze. Not a child in sight.

Lyn walked inside. The empty halls echoed her footsteps as she hurried to the principal's office. The school secretary pleasantly informed her that no one had seen Kristen since classes let out twenty-five minutes earlier.

Frantic with worry, Lyn drove around the school complex to the soccer fields in back. Her gaze skimmed the empty bleachers and short grass, looking for her cute little girl.

Nothing.

A cold, sick feeling settled in Lyn's stomach. She hadn't been to her office or checked in with Cindy all morning. After pulling to the side of the road, she flipped her phone open and jabbed the buttons to call her office manager. Surely Kristen wouldn't have walked all the way to her office by herself. Or home. Would she?

Lyn had given Kristen strict instructions never

to do such a thing. If she fell down and couldn't get up, she could be in big trouble. Kristen understood she was supposed to go inside the school and wait. But that didn't mean the girl would obey.

"I don't know where she is, but you better get over here fast," Cindy told her.

"Why? What's wrong?"

A blast of static stole Cindy's comment, but Lyn caught the word *picketers*. A word Lyn had come to dread over the expanse of her career. But nothing mattered more to her than Kristen's safety. Her child came first.

Lyn made a quick trip home, but found the door locked, no one there. Maybe she'd pass Kristen on the way back to her office. She drove the route slowly, glancing at rows of tidy houses, the grocery store and park. No sign of Kristen.

As she pulled into the parking lot at her office, Lyn blinked in disbelief. A crowd of people stood out front, waving a variety of colorful homemade signs. Perhaps fifty people, many wearing Native American dress, clogged the entrance to the building.

"Save the wild horses. Save the wild horses," they chanted in loud, singsong unison.

Two-by-two, the picketers paraded in front of the glass doors, the line meandering around the side of the building. They waved their signs, trying to draw attention. A cameraman and local news crew stood among the crowd, the reporter holding a microphone as she interviewed the protestors.

And smack-dab in the middle of the mob was Kristen, carrying a big colored sign that read I Love Wild Horses. No Roundups!

Lyn laughed at the irony of the situation. Then a sick feeling settled in her stomach. Her face blazed with betrayal and embarrassment. Kristen was safe. That was the important thing. But her own daughter was picketing her. And that stung Lyn's heart like nothing else could.

Lyn stepped out of her car, bracing herself for what was to come. Trying to settle the racing of her pulse. She looked for Cade among the protestors, but didn't see him. Oh, what she wouldn't say when she found him…

Kristen must have walked here from school. Her stamina had increased by leaps and bounds. Had she known about the demonstrators, or been drawn into their cause once she'd arrived? Did she even understand what she was doing? Either way, this wouldn't look good on the evening news. The forest ranger's own daughter picketing her.

If only Cade had warned Lyn about this exhibition. Neither of them had made any promises, but she thought they were better friends than this. His treachery scalded her face with heat. First he'd put Kristen on a horse, and now this.

Holding her head high, Lyn walked purposefully

toward the redbrick building. She ignored a trickle of sweat between her shoulder blades and tried to remember who she was and what she represented. Tried to remember to keep her cool, no matter what.

Billie Shining Elk separated himself from the crowd and stood on the hot pavement, arms folded across his beaded buckskin shirt. The regal majesty of a flowing white feather headdress sat perched low across his brow. His leathered face showed no sign of friendship, his black eyes slicing her in two.

As she approached, she met his gaze with a challenging lift of her chin. Refusing to back down. Refusing to cower before this man who had shown her no respect.

Standing in front of him, she looked up at his stoic face and spoke strong, but low. For his ears alone. "Chief Shining Elk, you can picket me anytime you want. But even you should agree it's not nice to involve my innocent little daughter in this activity. You should be ashamed of yourself."

He blinked. Just once. A glimmer of disgrace flashed in his gleaming eyes, then was gone. So fast, she thought she must have imagined it. But it was enough to know her words had hit home.

Pivoting on her heels, she walked to Kristen, ignoring the thronging crowd with their glares and taunts as they circled her like a pack of wolves. She felt like a cornered rabbit as they moved in for the kill.

"Hi, Mom!" Kristen greeted her with a blameless smile. She lowered her sign, resting the stick on the ground beside her feet.

Lyn knew her daughter well enough to know that the girl didn't realize what she was picketing. Not really. Not when Kristen's guileless expression showed such an earnest smile.

Lyn gritted her teeth, determined to keep her voice calm. "Hi, hon. You weren't at school when I went to pick you up just now. I was very worried about you."

"You were late." A thread of sullenness wavered in the girl's voice.

"I'm sorry, but you should have waited for me inside. Remember we've talked about this many times?"

"Sorry." Kristen's surly glare spoke volumes. She was anything but sorry for leaving.

"Please go inside and wait for me in my office. I need to speak with these people, and then I'll take you home."

The girl frowned. "But I wanna stay. I'm helping them picket."

"Yes, I can see that. But do you understand what you're picketing?"

"Yeah, they're trying to move wild horses like Lightning off the range. That's so mean, Mom. You can stop them, can't you?"

Lyn coughed. Though she wasn't getting along

with her child, Kristen thought she could help. Lyn would have found humor in the situation if it wasn't so serious. Obviously Kristen had no idea the picketers were protesting her own mother. And yet, if Kristen knew the full story, Lyn feared her daughter would picket her anyway.

"Why don't you leave her alone, Ranger? She knows where she belongs," someone jeered.

"Yeah, she knows what's right, even if you don't. Let her stay with us."

Lyn's heart beat faster. Kristen belonged with her. Mother and child. Always and forever. No matter what. They couldn't be separated. Not even in death.

Kristen's eyes widened in confusion. "What do they mean, Mom?"

Lyn placed her hand on her daughter's shoulder as she met the girl's eyes. "I need you to trust me right now, honey. I'm doing my best for everyone involved. Please go inside and wait for me. I'll explain everything to you in a few minutes. But first, I need to talk to these people. Okay?"

The girl's brow crinkled, and Lyn feared she might refuse. The last thing Lyn wanted was to have an argument with her child here on the street with all these people gawking. She hoped her daughter still trusted her enough to obey.

When the girl handed her sign off to a matronly woman next to her and headed for the door, Lyn breathed with relief. Kristen's actions reinforced what was most important to Lyn. Her fledgling faith in God and her child.

As the door closed behind Kristen, Lyn turned and faced the angry crowd.

"What's going on here?"

Cade jogged toward the throng of picketers, his gaze focused on Lyn as she stood among them. The drab olive-green of her ranger uniform stood out like a beacon, and the angry horde swarmed her. She wasn't a big woman and looked small and defenseless against the tall men packing a melee of signs. Yet she didn't back down.

If only Cade had found out about the protest an hour earlier, he might have been able to stop it. Maya's warning had come a bit too late. The stethoscope hanging around his neck bounced against the white smock he wore over his red chambray shirt. Having run all the way from his office four blocks away, he breathed deeply, trying to catch his breath.

"I think it's apparent what's going on." Lyn indicated the mass of people with her hand. "Are you responsible for this? Your people are picketing me. They think I've called for a roundup."

Cade's mouth dropped open. He'd feared something was up last night when the tribal council asked him to leave the meeting just after he'd given them his latest report on the wild horses. They'd planned to picket the forest ranger and hadn't told him about it. "No, Lyn. I didn't know anything about this."

She didn't seem to hear him. "How could you turn my own daughter against me, Cade? She's been picketing, too. Was that your plan all along? Using Kristen's physical therapy and Lightning to win her over to your cause so she could pressure me to leave the horses alone?"

Her eyes filled with anger and hurt. She'd trusted him. They'd become friends, yet it appeared that he'd betrayed her.

"No, Lyn. I'd never do that to you or Kristen. I didn't know about this. I'm innocent."

"Well, that's not how it looks to me. Maybe you better explain."

People were closing in on her, their faces filled with hostility. A protective feeling rose up inside of Cade, and he stepped in front of her. As if he could defend her against this angry horde. But he knew he'd try. No matter what the cost. To the death.

Because he loved her.

The realization struck him like a bolt of electricity. He loved her. Dal was right. Cade finally admitted it to himself. But how? How could he love a woman he barely knew?

And yet, he knew more than enough.

"I've been completely honest with you from the

very first," Lyn said. "I thought you'd been honest with me, too."

"I have, Lyn. I have."

If only she'd believe him.

"Then why this? You know I wouldn't call the BLM for a roundup without telling you about it first." She tossed a frustrated glare at Billie. "And you. I've sent a letter and called your office numerous times to ask for a meeting with your tribal council. Not once have you responded. Yet you show up here today with picketers and trick my daughter into helping you. What kind of a man does that?"

Cade blew out a breath as he looked at Chief Shining Elk. "Oh, Billie. What have you done?"

The chief's jaw clenched, hard as chiseled stone. He did have the good grace to look away, but he didn't apologize. He didn't say a word.

"Lyn, I'm sorry," Cade said. "I didn't know, or I would have warned you."

"That's why we didn't tell you," Billie growled at Cade. "We feared you'd been swayed by the woman. You have sided with her."

The woman! Referring to Lyn in such a manner seemed so demeaning to Cade. He didn't like it. Not at all.

"She's the forest ranger, Chief Shining Elk," Cade said. "Her gender has nothing to do with her work here. And I haven't sided with her. I just think we should work with the authorities if we want to do what's best for the mustangs. That's what I told you and the other tribal elders last night. But I think you've made this personal because of Clarisse."

Billie drew back as though he'd been struck in the face. His eyes narrowed in anger.

"Who is Clarisse?" Lyn asked.

Cade kept his gaze locked on Billie as he answered. "My mother."

Lyn shook her head. "What does she have to do with the wild horses?"

Cade didn't respond, but Billie's expression hardened, his eyes darkening to black daggers. For several tense moments, the two men glared at each other. The crowd quieted, watching and waiting. Finally, Billie looked away, ending the explosive moment.

"I've had it. You two can talk this out." Lyn spoke in a low, angry voice. "I'm going inside now. You can sit out here and picket me all you want. And once I've finished my study of the wild-horse situation, I'll make the best possible recommendation I can to the BLM. With or without your cooperation."

She turned and went inside, her long ponytail bouncing with her brisk stride. Cade's gaze followed every step. He'd witnessed her dedication to doing what was best for the mustangs. He couldn't fault her efforts. And yet, he knew that any wild horses not adopted by people who could care for them would be sent to holding stations where they'd live their lives in confinement.

And where did that leave him, Lyn and Kristen? Nowhere he wanted to be, that was for certain. His insides were a jumble of confusion. This situation had gotten out of his control.

"You used her daughter to help picket?" Cade asked the chief.

Billie's response was nothing more than a tight-lipped grunt.

"That's pretty low, don't you think?" Cade pressed.

No response. But Cade didn't expect one. He'd lost a lot of respect for the chief, and yet he felt sorry for Billie, too.

"Go home," Cade called to the crowd with a wave of his hand. "You're picketing the wrong office. The forest ranger isn't the one to decide if there'll be a roundup. That's up to the BLM. You shouldn't be here."

A murmur of doubt rose among the throng. He'd known each person most of his life. Many of them were his patients. They trusted him, for now. But this volatile issue could drive them away. He'd be lucky if he could keep his medical office open after this fiasco.

"The ranger's been trying to help us," Cade continued. "She's trying to save the mustangs. I've seen it with my own eyes. We need to work with the authorities, not against them."

Out of his peripheral vision, he caught a camera crew filming his every word.

Great. He'd be on the evening news. By tomorrow morning, the entire community would know about this nightmare.

"She only cares about the ranchers. She doesn't care about the wild horses!" a man yelled.

"Sure she does. I've been out riding with her and seen the work she's trying to do for the mustangs," Cade insisted.

He launched into a short dialogue on the things he'd seen and some of the tactics the Forest Service was using to try to combat the problem. For all the wildlife. Not just the mustangs. It was a duplicate of the report he'd given the tribal elders the night before.

"You don't know what you're talking about," one woman insisted. "Roundups kill wild horses. They drive the mustangs to death."

"They don't lose more than one percent of the horses," Cade said.

"That's one percent too many," a man called.

"And how many horses, deer and desert bighorn sheep will we lose if they can't find water and starve to death? Certainly more than one percent," he shot back.

A number of people jeered at Cade. They were

acting closed-minded and were unwilling to listen. It was like facing a brick wall of ignorance. He realized they didn't understand the environmental impacts resulting from overpopulated herds. How could they? They spoke from their hearts, not academic learning and experience.

Cade had heard enough. The picketers would have to do what they wanted. Turning, he headed back to his office. Dal met him at the corner where he'd been standing, listening to this dialogue. The two men fell into step together, walking in silence for half a block while Cade mulled over what he should do now. He needed to talk to Lyn. To explain things to her. To make her understand. But how should he proceed? By phone call or in person? Hopefully she wouldn't hang up on him or slam a door in his face.

"You think she'll ever speak to me again?" Cade finally asked his friend.

"Not unless you speak to her first. I advise taking flowers when you apologize. Maybe daisies. They'll get the message across, but won't come on too strong until you ask her out."

Cade shook his head. "Flowers? You don't get it, do you?"

Dal shrugged, giving him a lopsided grin. "Of course I do. You care for that woman, and she cares for you. Nothing else matters."

"That's not true. A lot matters here. This is a

serious situation. She's very angry right now. We're talking about her job. Flowers aren't gonna cut it."

"Then what will?"

Cade had no idea. It was just his luck that he'd finally met a woman he loved and wanted to be with, and they faced an impossible situation that would most likely destroy any happiness they might find together.

Silence loomed between the two men with just the sound of cars speeding past on the busy road. Cade turned away from the exhaust fumes, trying to think of a brilliant way to restore his relationship with Lyn. But once trust had been broken, it was harder to restore.

He'd always known this day might come. He and Lyn had been on opposite sides from the very first. And yet, part of his mind kept telling him they could agree to disagree on this issue. At least until the BLM hauled his beloved horses away.

Trust was the problem, and there were no easy answers. No matter what they did, someone was going to get hurt. Lyn might never believe in him again. And he couldn't blame her. He just didn't know how to repair the damage to their relationship.

Chapter Eleven

The following Saturday, Kristen sat at the kitchen table, staring out the window. Her eyes filled with gloomy resignation, she watched the vacant road, as though expecting to see someone there.

"What're you doing?" Lyn asked.

The girl turned and wiped her moist eyes, as though embarrassed to be caught crying. "Reading."

Lyn glanced at the closed book sitting on the table in front of her daughter. Reticent to cause an argument, Lyn almost turned back to the kitchen sink without comment.

Almost.

Something compelled her to dry her damp hands on a dish towel, then pull out a chair and sit beside her little girl. She'd explained about the picketers and wild horses and Kristen seemed to understand, but they hadn't talked much since that horrible day. Lyn didn't know how much longer they could go on like this. "You're not reading, honey. You're staring out the window and grieving. I'd like to know why."

Kristen blinked and ducked her head. Lyn braced herself to receive the silent treatment. Again.

"Do you think he'll ever come home?" The child's voice sounded low and choked with emotion.

"Who?" Lyn asked.

"Daddy."

A painful thud struck Lyn's heart. "No, hon. He can't. You know Dad's in heaven now."

Kristen licked her lips, looking small and exposed. "Dal came back. The doctors declared him dead and he lost a leg like me, but he lived. He came back home. He doesn't let anything stand in his way."

Taking a deep inhale, Lyn released it on a sigh. "Unfortunately your dad's body was too damaged for him to live. He can't come back, sweetheart. But I know we'll see him again. I know if he could have come home, he would have."

Kristen lifted her head, her eyes swimming with tears. "Did I do something bad to make him go away?"

Lyn's heart squeezed painfully, and she wrapped her arms around her child. "Oh, no, honey. Not at all. He just died. It wasn't anything you did. He loved you so very much. I know he would have stayed with us if he could. He didn't want to leave, I can promise you that. He loved his life. He loved us."

For the first time in a long time, Kristen hugged her mother back. Liquid warmth pooled in Lyn's chest, and she couldn't stop the flow of tears. She held her daughter for long, tender minutes while they both cried. And when Lyn sat back, Kristen smiled at her. She actually smiled.

"Thanks, Mom. I feel better."

"So do I."

The timer buzzed, announcing the cake in the oven had finished baking. Lyn stood and reached for the hot pads before opening the oven. The sweet, tantalizing aroma flooded the kitchen. When Kristen let out a happy squeal, Lyn almost dropped the hot pan on the tiled floor.

"Cade's here!" The girl bounced happily in her seat and waved, but couldn't stand because she wasn't wearing her prosthesis.

The doorbell rang, and Lyn's heart gave a quick stutter.

"I'll get it." Setting the cake on a cooling rack, Lyn padded into the living room in bare feet. Taking a deep breath, she opened the door. Just as Kristen had said, Cade stood before her.

"Hi, there. These are for you." His lips twitched as though he tried to smile but failed. He opened the screen door, lifting a bouquet of white daisies toward her.

He'd brought her flowers?

"Hello," she answered, not taking the gift.

She knew what this was. An apology. Something she didn't want from him. Something she didn't dare accept. Even knowing he had nothing to do with the picketers, she was still angry and not at all certain she should continue her friendship with this man. Something told her it would only lead to more trouble and disappointment.

A rustling sounded in the kitchen, and she glanced over her shoulder. Kristen balanced herself against the wall as she hopped on one leg to retrieve her prosthesis from the coffee table.

"Can I speak with you outside?" Lifting a hand, Lyn pushed lightly against Cade's chest as she stepped out onto the porch with him. She closed the door quietly behind her. He glanced down at her pink toenails.

"How are you feeling today?" he asked.

"I'm fine. What do you want?" she asked, trying not to let bitterness clog her voice.

His smile wilted, replaced by a regretful gaze as he met her eyes. "I had to see you again. To tell you how sorry I am. I couldn't leave things as they were. Not without knowing you and Kristen were all right."

"We're fine. You can leave now." She turned toward the door.

"Please, Lyn." He gave her arm a gentle tug, pulling her back around.

Crossing her arms, she released a deep sigh. Why wouldn't he leave them alone?

"Billie has a vendetta against me," he said. "I think that's why he didn't tell me he was planning to picket your office."

"What do you mean?"

He shrugged one incredibly broad shoulder. "You remember I told you the elders wanted my mother to marry a member of the tribe? But she loved my father and married him instead."

Lyn nodded, wondering what this had to do with the picketing.

"Billie Shining Elk was the man the tribe wanted her to marry. When she refused and eloped with my dad, it brought shame to Billie. He's never forgiven me for it."

"But why? It wasn't your fault your mother loved and married another man."

"It doesn't matter. Billie blames me."

"That was years ago, and you're his doctor."

A half smile curved Cade's full lips. "Yeah, it's kind of ironic, huh? He hates me, but he still comes to my office because there isn't another doctor in town. And yet, he won't take the medicines I prescribe. He thinks I'm trying to poison him. Sometimes I think Billie is his own worst enemy."

She laughed—she couldn't help it. People could be so silly. But knowing the truth didn't change much between her and Cade. Not really.

"I want you to have these." He pressed the bouquet of flowers against her palm.

Weary of this battle, she wrapped her fingers around the leafy stems, the green paper crackling. It'd been so long since a man had given her flowers. Even if these were just a peace offering, she couldn't resist.

"Thank you."

He stepped closer. "Can't we still be friends? I'm hoping you'll bring Kristen out to the ranch soon. I've bought a new gelding that Dal is training to ride. We could make a day of it, complete with a picnic."

A picnic. With Cade Baldwin. It sounded so... so domestic. And fun. Kristen would love it. The June weather was unseasonably warm. Lyn could take the opportunity to check on the water hole near Emmitt's Point. And they could... No! Lyn couldn't be sucked in by this man again. No more.

"Dal is training the horse?" The resiliency of both men surprised Lyn. They were quite a pair, and she couldn't help admiring Cade in spite of everything standing between them.

"Yeah, he grew up on a ranch in Oklahoma. I'd

like to resume physical therapy with Kristen again, if you'll agree. No horse riding this time. I promise."

She hissed a breath of exasperation. "Cade, I don't think we can—"

"Can I please come in?" He hurried on as though trying to intercept her refusal. "I'd like to give Kristen an update on Lightning. I've weaned the filly off the bottle. She's eating hay like a pig and getting bigger every day."

Lyn couldn't help chuckling at that. Oh, she was tempted to agree. Both she and Kristen loved that little horse. No doubt Kristen almost had her prosthesis on by now. At any moment, the girl would barge through the door, eager to see Cade. Hearing about the filly would lead to more visits to the ranch. Which would bring them near Cade again. Which would win Lyn more condemnation from his tribe. No matter what, she was the forest ranger and Cade was a wild-horse advocate. They just didn't see eye to eye on this issue. And honestly, Lyn didn't think her heart could take being near Cade anymore. He'd become too important in her life. He'd come to mean so much to both her and Kristen.

Too much.

"I don't think that's wise, Cade. I'll always be grateful for everything you've done for Kristen, but I think it's best if we just part ways now." She lifted her gaze to gauge his reaction.

The crease in his forehead deepened. "Please don't say that, Lyn. We can work this out. The wild horses have nothing to do with you, me and Kristen. Not really. They're just a cause we both care a great deal about."

She snorted. "They have everything to do with us, Cade."

"Not if we don't let it."

What exactly was he saying? She didn't dare ask. It would only lead to more heartache or embarrassment. Because now she wanted more from their relationship than just friends, and she didn't think she or Kristen were ready for that. Maybe in another year or two.

Maybe never.

"We were just working together, Cade. Nothing more." Maybe if she said the words often enough, she'd actually come to believe them.

He licked his lips. "I'd still like us to be friends."

It was so hard to ignore his plea, but she saw no other way. And now she must reveal the big clincher. "You should know the BLM contacted me yesterday afternoon. The director saw the evening news with all the picketers in front of the Forest Service office. Since the mustangs cross boundary lines, the BLM is already aware of the problem and has scheduled a roundup for next month. It's out of my hands. I didn't have to call them after all. They're having a roundup anyway."

A long, swelling silence followed.

"I'm sorry to hear that. Foaling season will be ending the first week in July. They'll be running young foals. They could be running expectant mothers who are late in dropping their foals. They could lose their babies." His words sounded wooden. Hurt.

"Yes, there's always the chance of that, but the contractor has promised not to fly the helicopters faster than the slowest animal. I know this particular contractor out of Utah. He's one of the best."

Cade snorted. "Yeah, and we all know how that works out. Some of those babies literally run their hooves off. They're not strong yet. Their little hooves slough off, and then they have to be put down."

"I'm sorry, Cade. I've done everything I could. I hope you know that. Sometimes there are just no easy answers. Not in a situation like this."

"Yes, I know. But I hate to see any creature locked away when they want to be free."

"I do, too. But…why is this so important to you, Cade? It's like you're personally responsible for the mustangs. I don't understand."

She shouldn't have asked, but couldn't help herself. Dal had mentioned that Cade had suffered more than the other men at war, and she wanted to know why.

His expression darkened, his eyes filled with subtle rebellion. "You really want to know?"

"Yes." At least, she thought she did. But his hushed voice sent a shiver of apprehension down her spine.

"I was a prisoner of war for twenty-one days, Lyn. Not very long when compared to other prisoners, but long enough to endure some unspeakable things. I was finally rescued. In the process, Dal lost his leg. To save me. And that's all I'm ever gonna say about it again."

So now she knew. He hadn't spelled out the gritty details, but her mind filled in the blanks. The knife scars she'd noticed on his neck, chest and arms. The haunted look in his eyes when he'd had to destroy the injured mare. The strong friendship he shared with Dallin Savatch. It all made sense.

They were brothers in arms. They'd given so much for their country. And for each other. They both deserved some peace.

"I'm so very sorry, Cade." And she meant it. She could only imagine what he must have suffered. What he had endured. She hated the thought of anyone torturing him. Keeping him prisoner.

No wonder he loved the mustangs so much. And yet, he still tried to do the right things.

He reached out and cupped her cheek with his

hand. The warmth of his calloused palm sent shock waves through her.

"It's okay now. The Lord brought me home," he said. "What I went through made me who I am today. I'm so blessed to be alive, and I owe God so much."

So did Lyn. For so long, she'd looked at the car accident and losing Rob with such bitterness. She'd seen no good that had come from it. Kristen losing her leg. All the pain and anguish that had followed. Walking the floors of the hospital, wondering if her child would survive. Endless therapy sessions. Endless tears. And yet, Lyn could no longer blame God. It wasn't His fault a drunk driver had hit them. It was the drunk driver's fault. Recovering hadn't been easy, but the Lord had brought them through. Her faith had been growing every day, and she no longer wanted to be angry at God anymore.

But that changed nothing between her and Cade.

She turned her face to the side, and he dropped his hand away.

"I'd like to participate in the roundup. Just to ensure the horses are treated humanely," he said.

She nodded. "I can arrange that. You can ride with me."

"You'll be there?"

"Yes. Like you, I want to make sure the chopper doesn't run any expectant mares or young foals into the ground. Don't worry. Some of the healthy mares will receive a fertility vaccination and then be released back into the wild. Other horses will be made available to the public for adoption to good homes."

A frustrated sigh whispered past his lips. "There are never enough people willing to adopt the mustangs. Too many horses end up imprisoned for the rest of their lives in holding facilities. That isn't humane, either."

"It's better than the mustangs slowly starving to death." She hesitated. "Maybe you should adopt some of them. Dal could train them for you. You could open a horse camp for amputee children out at Sunrise Ranch. You're a doctor and have the medical knowledge. And you certainly have room in that big house of yours."

Why had she suggested such a thing? The words poured out of her mouth before she could stop them. She was being half-sarcastic, half-serious. And yet, the thought was a good one, but expensive. Even with his medical degree and background in prosthetics, Cade might not have the resources to take on such a big project. Besides, he wanted to start up an outfitters business and guide people into the deepest parts of the wilderness, not begin a horse camp for amputee kids.

When he didn't respond, she didn't press the issue. It wasn't her business what he did or who adopted the mustangs.

Cade tilted his head, his eyes creased at the corners as though he was thinking about her suggestion. "It's good to see you, Lyn. Tell Kristen I said hello. And my offer stands. You're both welcome in my home and medical office. Anytime."

Turning, he walked across the porch. His boot heels pounded the wood as he hurried down the steps. Lyn appreciated his kind words, knowing they must have been difficult for him. As difficult as it was for her to let him go.

As he backed his truck out of the driveway, the front door jerked open and Kristen gasped. "He's leaving already? Without saying hello?"

Lyn nodded, his flowers hanging limp in her hand as she held them upside down beside her leg. "He couldn't stay, but he brought these flowers for you. He had to leave."

Because of her.

Watching him drive away was one of the hardest things Lyn had ever done. Turning, she handed the daisies to her daughter, then went back inside the house. Kristen followed much later.

That afternoon, Lyn received another surprise visit. She'd enticed Kristen to go outside and help her water the clay flower pots lining the front porch. As Kristen showered pink and white petunias with the watering can, Lyn playfully squirted the girl's bare foot with the garden hose. To Lyn's surprise, Kristen giggled and tossed a handful of water back at her.

Raucous laughter ensued. Finally. And it felt good after lying dormant for so long.

Lyn turned off the water and coiled the hose near the outside tap. A white minivan pulled up out front. Wiping her damp hands down the sides of her blue capris, Lyn stepped onto the freshly mowed lawn. She'd worked hard today, missing the strength and comfort of a man in her life.

Missing Cade in spite of sending him away.

"Who's that?" Sitting on the top porch step, Kristen shielded her eyes against the bright glare of sunlight.

Lyn shook her head. "I have no idea."

A tall, balding man got out of the van and waved, then hurried around the vehicle, where he opened the back hatch. A woman with short, red hair and a thick waist got out of the passenger seat and gave them a timid smile.

Conscious of Kristen pulling herself up to a standing position, Lyn sauntered over to the sidewalk.

"May I help you?" she asked.

The woman slid a back door open, revealing a little boy not much older than Kristen, belted into his seat. Lyn's gaze immediately dropped to the child's legs. Or leg. The left one was missing. His pair of knee-length shorts hung limp on that side, his stump wrapped in white bandages.

Lyn's breath hitched inside her throat, and compassion blanketed her. Another amputee child.

"My name's Martin Lewis." The man held out his hand. "This is my wife, Sharon. And this is our son, Matt."

Lyn took the man's hand and smiled in greeting. She figured they'd heard about Kristen and wanted to meet her. Group therapy was important for children to mingle with other amputee kids, but neither Cade nor Lyn knew of any other youngsters in the area whom Kristen could spend time with. Maybe that was about to change.

"I'm glad to meet you. I'm Lyn Warner, and this is my daughter, Kristen." Lyn jerked her thumb toward her daughter, who joined them, walking like an expert.

Almost in unison, Martin's and Sharon's gazes dropped to Kristen's C-Leg prosthesis showing beneath the cuffed hem of her shorts.

"Hello, Kristen." Sharon smiled, her cheeks plumping.

"Hi." Kristen gave a shy wave.

The boy grinned, the bridge of his freckled nose crinkling. Though slim like his dad, Matt had his mother's auburn hair. "Hi, there."

Martin folded out the wheelchair and lifted Matt into the seat. "I hope we're not intruding. We tried to call before we dropped by unannounced, but no one answered the phone."

"We've been working outside most of the afternoon and probably didn't hear the phone ring. It's no problem," Lyn reassured them.

Kristen gravitated to Matt, standing close, but not comfortable enough to speak freely yet.

"We're from Winnemucca," Martin explained. "I work for the State Fish and Game office. One of your employees told us about you yesterday. We couldn't wait to take a drive and meet you."

Winnemucca was a small Nevada town about a two-hour drive to the east. Not a real long distance, but far enough away that Lyn was impressed by their eagerness.

"May I ask who told you about us?" Lyn asked.

The neighbor across the street started up their Weed Eater, and Sharon spoke louder over the noise. "Cindy Halston. She's my first cousin on my mother's side."

"She's my office manager," Lyn said.

Like Kristen, Matt now belonged to a club of amputee kids he didn't want to belong to. But being together helped the children realize they weren't alone.

"Yes, we know." Martin's grin widened as if he were relieved to have the introductions over with.

"Won't you come sit on the porch in the shade?"

Lyn asked, feeling confident this family wasn't a danger to her or Kristen.

"Thank you." Sharon stepped past Lyn and joined Kristen while Martin pushed Matt's wheelchair up the path. Lyn hurried to retrieve a wooden ramp she always set over the stairs whenever Kristen used her wheelchair, which was infrequent these days.

Martin pushed Matt's chair up the ramp. The wheels thumped as they hit the porch. They all sat in wicker chairs while Lyn went inside to the kitchen and retrieved a cold pitcher of lemonade from the fridge. After collecting glasses, ice and a plate of chocolate-chip cookies, she carried the refreshments back out on a plastic tray and poured everyone a cool drink.

"How old are you?" Kristen asked the boy.

"I just turned twelve."

"I'm ten. When did you lose your leg?"

"About five months ago. It got tangled in a hay chopper," Matt said. "How'd you lose yours?"

"In a car crash. My dad died in the accident, too."

A jagged thatch of red hair fell over Matt's brow, and he pushed it back. "Gee, I'm sorry. Does your stump still hurt?"

Kristen shook her head. "Not anymore, but sometimes I still have phantom pain. I just massage the stump, and it soon feels better."

Phantom pain…the feeling that her missing leg was still there. Cade had mentioned it once during a therapy session, but Kristen never complained about it to Lyn. It seemed Kristen had confided in everyone except her mom.

Until today.

"Have you started walking yet?" Kristen asked.

Matt nodded. "But it hurts a lot."

The adults listened with rapt attention as the kids talked, anxious to hear every response. Kristen and Matt were so eager to share their experience with someone who understood what they were going through.

"Give it time," Kristen said. "Pretty soon, you'll be getting around all by yourself. You should go see Dr. Baldwin. He's the best doctor in the world. He helped me walk better, and I can even run now. You almost can't tell I'm an amputee."

To prove her point, she stood and walked across the porch with barely a hitch.

Tears burned the backs of Lyn's eyes as she watched her daughter's confident stride. Her beautiful, courageous girl. Kristen had overcome this horrible obstacle not because of Lyn, but in spite of her. When she glanced at Sharon, Lyn found the other woman wiping her eyes, too.

"We'd love to meet Dr. Baldwin." Sharon's voice sounded hoarse with emotion. "Cindy told us he's worked wonders with you. She said he uses horse therapy to strengthen your legs and back. Our Mattie loves horses, and we want him to be able to ride again."

Lyn fought off a shudder of fear. How could Sharon stand to let her son ride after all he'd been through? Surely the woman was scared of Matt being hurt again. Wasn't she?

"We can take you," Kristen offered eagerly. "Dr. Baldwin lets us visit his ranch anytime we want. He's keeping my horse out at his place."

Lyn tensed, knowing where this was leading. She didn't know if she was up to another visit with Cade today.

"You can do anything you want," Kristen told Matt, her expression and voice filled with optimism. "Don't let your amputation stop you. I ride horses and even play soccer…or at least I used to." She tossed a dismissive glance toward Lyn.

Matt's eyes widened. "You really think I can ride again?"

"Of course. Why not?"

Why not? The words sank deep into Lyn's heart. And suddenly all the fears and excuses she'd made as to why Kristen shouldn't ride no longer made sense. Not at the expense of her daughter's happiness. Not if it kept Kristen from doing what fulfilled her.

Not if it kept the girl from living a happy life.

"I just knew this visit would do our Mattie good." Martin showed a toothy grin as he bit into a cookie.

Lyn chewed her bottom lip, not knowing how to reply. She only knew how she felt. Petty and small. Seeing her daughter so confident and enthusiastic, Lyn wondered why she'd ever denied Kristen the opportunity to ride. When they'd first moved to Stokely, Kristen had seemed so hesitant and insecure. Now the girl was offering encouragement to Matt. Strong and positive. And just like that, a flood of understanding swept over Lyn. Yes, it was safer for Kristen on the ground. Safer not to try. But what was life without joy? The Lord didn't want His children to be sad. He wanted them to be happy. Cade's deep faith in God had taught Lyn that much. So what right did Lyn have to keep Kristen from reaching her full potential? What right did she have to keep her girl from trying?

None at all.

Kristen rested her hand on the push handle of Matt's chair. "Dr. Baldwin's place isn't very far. We can take you out there today, can't we, Mom?"

Everyone stared at Lyn, awaiting her response. From the affirmative expressions on each face, Lyn knew they all wanted to go. What could she say? Especially since she wanted to go, too.

"Um, sure. I'd be happy to take you out and introduce you to Dr. Baldwin." She stood, surprised when Martin and Sharon hopped to their feet. Their eagerness spoke volumes. Like Lyn, they wanted to help their child in any way they could. They wanted Matt to be happy.

While Lyn took the glasses and tray inside and set them in the sink, the Lewises laughed and chatted with the children. After retrieving her purse and keys, Lyn went back outside. Martin already had Matt buckled in his seat, and Sharon was just stowing the boy's chair in the back of the van.

What would Cade say when they showed up on his doorstep? How could Lyn explain seeing him again so soon? She didn't know what she should say.

Kristen sat next to Matt, but Lyn didn't feel comfortable letting her daughter ride alone with these strangers. At least, not yet.

"Honey, come ride with me in our car. You can help me show the Lewises how to get out to Sunrise Ranch." Having said the words, Lyn held her breath, hoping Kristen agreed without a fight.

"Okay." The girl slid out of the van, got her balance and walked to their sedan parked nearby.

Again, Lyn couldn't help feeling pleasantly surprised by her daughter's progress. Kristen's movements were so fluid and smooth. So graceful.

Both Sharon and Martin stared after the girl, their eyes filled with amazement. And envy.

No doubt, they wanted this ease of walking for

their own son. Lyn couldn't blame them. And she had Cade to thank for it all.

Cade, whom she'd shunned.

As Lyn started the engine and backed her car out of the driveway, an overwhelming warmth enveloped her. A feeling that flowed through her limbs, chest and head. A feeling of absolute peace.

Taking these people to meet Cade was the right thing to do. Lyn knew that without a doubt. But something must change in her and Kristen's lives. And soon. Lyn just needed to sort it all out.

Chapter Twelve

"Lyn! I didn't expect to see you again so soon." Cade leaned his arms against the rim of her open car window and smiled, unable to pretend indifference. A sad melancholy had shadowed him since he'd left her house earlier that morning. Knowing the BLM planned a horse roundup frustrated him. And yet, he felt slightly better knowing Lyn would be there with him to ensure humane treatment of the mustangs.

Because he trusted her. Because he loved her.

She'd parked beside his truck in the graveled driveway at his ranch. He'd been cleaning out the watering trough, his pulse speeding into overdrive the moment he spied her car coming down the road. Filled with happy energy, he'd hopped over the rail fence and joined her as she lowered her window.

"Hi, Dr. Baldwin." Kristen unlocked her seat belt and flashed a wide grin from where she sat beside her mom in the front seat.

"Hi, sweetie." He couldn't resist the cute little girl. He loved her, too. Like his own child.

But what were they doing here? He thought he'd never see them again, except perhaps sometimes when they happened to come across each other in town.

A white minivan pulled up behind Lyn's sedan, and a man Cade didn't recognize got out of the vehicle.

"Actually, we're not staying," Lyn said. "We're here on business. I just want to ask if—"

Kristen shoved the car door open, swung her legs around to the ground and thrust herself into a standing position.

"Kristen, wait," Lyn called.

The girl paid her mother no heed. Cade stepped back and waited for Kristen to walk to him. He accepted her hug, beyond relieved they were here, but not liking the way the girl ignored her mom.

"Your mother wants you." He pointed at Lyn and the child turned that way, a frown of dread marring her sweet features. No matter what, Cade thought Kristen should mind her mother. He would never subvert Lyn again. Not ever.

"Never mind. Go ahead." Lyn lifted a hand in dismissal.

Dal came from the barn, leading a bareback gelding. Kristen gave a shriek of joy and hurried

toward the marine. After tying the horse to the
hitching post, Dal greeted the girl.

"Howdy, pardner. You gonna ride today?"

Kristen shook her head. "Mom won't let me."

"Who are your friends?" Dal looked at the people emerging from the van.

Cade caught Lyn's disgruntled sigh behind him.
He had no time to make amends as Kristen introduced him to the Lewis family and explained what
they were doing here. Though he focused on Matt,
Cade was highly aware of Lyn as she opened her
car door. She extended a long, slender leg from the
vehicle and stood, dressed in knee-length capris
and a pair of white sandals. Out of his peripheral
vision, Cade caught the flash of pink nail polish on
her toes. Dainty, cute feet. But her shoes weren't
at all practical for a barnyard.

"So, you want to meet Lightning?" Cade asked
Matt.

"Sure!" the boy responded eagerly. A good sign,
considering he wasn't yet walking well.

Cade threw a smile in Lyn's direction, then followed as Kristen led the way to the barn. Lyn
brought up the rear, quiet and somber. Either she
didn't want to be here, or she had something heavy
on her mind.

Probably a mixture of both.

Over the course of the next forty minutes, Cade
and Dal gave the Lewis clan a tour of the place.

Kristen helped, her jolly stride and exuberant laugh oozing a slightly hyper excitement.

Under Dal's supervision, the kids fed and petted the filly. Cade enjoyed their laughter as they admired the wiry horse. For a few minutes, the children were able to forget they were different. That they didn't have legs, and they walked different from normal kids. Here, at Sunrise Ranch, it didn't matter. They were happy. They were wanted. They belonged. And Cade wished he could do the same for so many other amputee kids.

Martin and Sharon asked numerous questions about Cade's work. They explained Matt's amputation and described his current medical treatment.

"You think you could work with our son the way you've done with Kristen?" Martin asked.

"We can sure try. Give my office a call to set up an appointment." Cade reached into the front pocket of his Western shirt and pulled out a business card, which he handed to Sharon. He wouldn't make any promises until he'd had time to formally examine Matt and study his medical files.

"Lightning's getting really big," Kristen exclaimed. "Isn't she beautiful?"

"Yes," Matt agreed, his eyes glowing with admiration. The small horse was just the right size as the boy sat in his chair and ran his hands over the filly's smooth neck.

"Let me show you Magpie," Kristen offered.

She tried to thrust Matt's wheelchair through the mire of soft dirt, but the wheels bottomed out and Dal had to help push them forward. Watching them, Cade couldn't help clicking off mental calculations as to how he might make his ranch more wheelchair friendly. He'd listened that morning when Lyn suggested he start a horse camp for amputee children, and he wondered why he'd never thought of it before. When he'd suggested the idea to Dal, the marine eagerly offered to help.

Just one problem: after the roundup, Cade would love to buy a number of the younger wild horses for training, but he didn't have the funds to convert his ranch to accommodate amputee kids. Now he couldn't stop thinking of ways to overcome these obstacles.

"Cade, can I speak with you alone for a moment?"

He turned, pleased to find Lyn standing close beside him, her brow curved in a thoughtful frown. "Sure. What's on your mind?"

They stepped outside, the afternoon sunlight shimmering across her golden hair. His gaze lowered to the pulse beating in her smooth, white throat. How he loved her.

"I...I want to apologize to you," Lyn said.

He shook his head. "You don't owe me an apology, Lyn. Really. It's me who should apologize to you."

"Yes, I do. I...I realize now how wrong I was about your physical therapy methods. I've been living in fear the past year. I've held on so tight to Kristen that I've almost strangled her. I didn't realize how important it is to let her try new things and live and grow. You were right, and I was wrong. If it's okay, I'd like to resume her physical therapy with you."

Cade stared into her honey-brown eyes. A warm, tender feeling overwhelmed him. It must have taken a lot for Lyn to admit these things. And he admired her for pushing aside her fears and doing what was best for her child. No longer could he deny his love for her. And Kristen. If only he could break through the barriers guarding Lyn's broken heart.

If only she could love him in return.

"Of course it's okay," he said. He touched her cheek gently with his fingertips, delighted when she didn't pull away.

"And..." she swallowed hard "...it's okay by me if you let her ride horses, too. You should know I've made arrangements with the BLM to buy Lightning from them legally as part of the roundup. Kristen can ride, as long as you keep a watchful eye on her. I don't want her to get bucked off."

His mouth dropped open in shock. He hadn't

expected this concession. Not at all. "That's great. I promise to watch over her. I care about you both. Very much. No mustangs or roundups will ever change that, Lyn. Not for me."

And he meant it. Though he loved the wild horses, he loved Lyn and Kristen more. He might not always agree with Lyn's opinions, but he knew she'd tried to do right by the horses. Her professionalism and expertise would allow for nothing less. Because they respected one another, they could agree to disagree on many issues.

She released an unsteady breath and stepped back, seeming suddenly withdrawn. "Thanks, Cade. I really appreciate it. I'll call your office on Monday morning to set up our next appointment."

"That'll be fine."

Oh, couldn't he say something better than that? She'd just agreed to let him be Kristen's doctor again, complete with horse therapy. What more could he ask for?

Nothing, except her love.

As she walked toward the barn, he longed to call her back. To ask when he could see her again. Weekly therapy was fine, but he wanted so much more. He enjoyed being Kristen's doctor, but it wasn't enough. Not anymore. Not for him. He wanted them to be together every day. Like a real family. But that was just a dream. An illusion. Unless he could convince Lyn differently.

If only he dared tell Lyn his true feelings without driving her away again. But he couldn't. Not unless he wanted to lose her for good this time. Weekly physical therapy wasn't much, but he'd take anything he could get.

At least for now.

"I've made arrangements for you to return to Cade for your physical therapy," Lyn told Kristen as they drove home an hour later.

A long pause ensued while her words sank in. Then—

"Do you mean it, Mom?" the girl shrieked.

Lyn nodded, keeping her gaze on the road. "Yes, I mean it. I've already spoken to Cade about it."

"Oh, thanks, Momma. I can't wait." Jerking against her seat belt, Kristen leaned across the seat and hugged Lyn tight.

Lyn released one hand on the steering wheel long enough to hug her daughter back. She laughed, trying to focus on the dirt road and feeling as though a load of bricks had just fallen off her shoulders. "I thought you'd be pleased. Just be careful when you ride, okay?"

Kristen stared. "You mean I can ride horses again, too?"

Another nod. Another happy screech. Another tight squeeze.

"Oh, I'll be so careful, Mom. I promise." Kristen

sat back and smiled wide, her slender body wriggling with delight.

"I've worked everything out with Dr. Baldwin. He'll help you to be careful. And you're going to play soccer again, too."

"Really? Oh, I love you, Mom."

This time, the hug didn't end quickly. Lyn pulled over on the narrow road, wanting to share this rare affection with her child. Wanting it to go on forever.

They sat there for several moments with Lyn brushing her hand over Kristen's long, soft hair. Lyn tried to absorb the emotions flowing through her, but just couldn't contain the love she felt for her daughter. Thinking about the possible dangers involved, that old, familiar panic rose upward in Lyn's throat, but she forced it down. She couldn't stifle Kristen anymore. She had to let go, at least a little bit.

She must have faith.

"I'm so sorry I was hard on you, honey," Lyn whispered before placing a kiss on Kristen's forehead. "I didn't realize how much I was hurting you. I was so afraid you might get injured. I thought I was protecting you. You see, I love you so much. After we lost Dad, I was so frightened I might lose you, too. And maybe letting you ride reminded me that Dad wasn't here to ride with you."

Kristen sniffled, her fingers coiled around the

fabric of Lyn's cotton shirt. "I know, Mom. I was afraid, too. That…that you didn't love me anymore be-because Daddy died."

"Why would you think that?"

"Because it was my fault. If we hadn't been going to see that horse Daddy wanted to buy for me, he'd still be alive."

"Oh, no, honey. I've never thought that and never will. The accident wasn't your fault. Not at all. I just wish I'd gone and bought the horse after the accident. We were thrown into a horrible situation, but your dad wanted that horse for you. So now I'm going to make it up to you. You need Lightning. We both do. To remember your father and how much he loved us both." Lyn pressed her hand beneath Kristen's chin and lifted the girl's face so she could look into her eyes.

A giant tear rolled down the child's face, and Lyn wiped it away with the pad of her thumb.

"I love you so much," Lyn vowed. "Nothing can ever change that. I'll always be here for you, no matter what."

"I love you, too, Mom."

They sat huddled together for several moments, the murmuring wind the only sound for miles around.

"I'll always love Daddy, but I sure wish Cade could be a part of our family now," Kristen said.

Lyn stilled, her mind frozen on that thought. It was too soon to love another man.

Wasn't it?

"Cade will always be our special friend," Lyn conceded.

"It's not the same thing," Kristen said.

Yeah, Lyn knew that, too. But she just didn't know if she was ready for more.

"Come on. Let's go home." Lyn sat up straight and reached for the key. As she started the ignition, Kristen returned to her seat, her expression more serene. More secure and content.

Happy.

Lyn eased the car back onto the road, listening as Kristen chatted about the new soccer gear she'd need and her plans to help Dal train Lightning to stand at a tie beside the fence post.

A flutter of nervousness filled Lyn's stomach. She knew she'd made the right decision to return Kristen to Cade and let her ride. For the first time in a year, she understood her child and felt close to Kristen. They'd reconciled and were mother and child, as well as friends, again.

But where did that leave Lyn and Cade?

Nowhere. Cade was Kristen's doctor, nothing more. Lyn had too many obstacles in her life. Her profession. Her amputee daughter. Her broken heart.

Even if Cade were interested in her, Lyn couldn't

foist her complicated life on him. She didn't need another love. She'd regained her faith in God. She had enough to fill up her life. Didn't she?

So why couldn't she stop thinking about Cade?

Chapter Thirteen

The day of the wild-horse roundup, Cade heard the whir of the helicopter before he saw it. And then the thundering beat of hooves sifted across the valley—a low pounding of the earth that seemed to keep time with the beat of his heart.

Sitting astride Flash on the top of a hill far away, Cade used high-powered binoculars to look toward the east. Lyn sat beside him on Apple, alternately gazing through her own pair of binoculars and snapping pictures with her camera.

Clouds of dust spread over the scrubby rabbit brush and sage covering the vast expanse of Secret Valley. The chopper lifted into the sky, sunlight glinting off its silver skids as it whipped dirt and gravel across the desert floor.

Cade liked this strategic position where they wouldn't startle the horses, yet he and Lyn had an unobstructed view of the entire proceedings.

The chopper moved with slow purpose, invading the comfort zone of a band of mustangs. In response, the horses ran forward. To keep them from stampeding, the pilot pulled back a bit. In response, the horses settled into a gentle trot. Forward, backward. Working to keep just enough pressure on the horses that they'd move in the direction of the capture corral, without exhausting the weak and younger members of their band.

A shrill whinny, along with snorts and grunts, filled the air—a low commotion that grew louder the nearer the mustangs came to the pens, like the engine of a locomotive. The mustangs traveled the well-known path they usually took to water. They didn't know they were in danger of being captured.

Not yet.

"That's Beeswax." Lyn pointed as a honey-colored palomino sprinted over the steep swell of rocks a quarter of a mile away.

The flock of horses followed, a mixture of duns and bays, some with jagged blazes down their noses. They were obviously related to one another.

Cade made mental calculations. Eleven, twelve, thirteen mares, Beeswax, another blue roan stallion and two young foals. Both of them colts. With creamy coats and long, firm legs built for running.

"I think we've got two separate bands of horses here," he observed.

The horses trotted fast, the foals running to keep

up. But not enough to endanger the babies by pushing them too hard. The fact that the colts never fell behind testified to the expertise of the pilot. He didn't press the mustangs beyond their endurance, though Cade knew the horses ran harder as they neared the capture corral. That was when the chopper closed in to keep its quarry from turning back as they entered the wings of the trap. Young, weak or injured animals sometimes fell behind. That was what Cade and Lyn were here for. Outriders to help collect the stragglers.

The chopper worked the herd in an easy manner, which caused less stress on the mustangs. It wasn't always this way. Last year, Cade had watched a helicopter drive several mustangs into the ground. Expectant mares miscarried, and healthy foals dropped dead of exhaustion. Just as Lyn had promised, it appeared this contractor was more humane, obeying the policies and not pushing the horses beyond their stamina.

"Even with the two herds meshed together, they all look strong," Lyn remarked.

Resting one gloved hand on the cantle of her saddle, she gripped the reins in her other hand. Her voice sounded anxious, her eyes filled with urgency as she scanned the oncoming horde.

"Yeah." Cade remembered that time on the mountain when Lyn had named each of the stallions for him. Beeswax was always agitated and into everyone else's business. A serrated scar marred his hindquarters where a mountain lion may have clawed him years earlier. The mustang had escaped danger before. Would he do it again?

As Cade watched the proceedings, no panic set in. No breathless fear. No horrifying memories of war overwhelmed him. Just peace. Though he didn't want the wild horses rounded up, he hadn't seen any abusive treatment by the wranglers. Just lots of lean mustangs who needed food and water. And they'd get it as soon as they arrived at the capture corral. Like having your teeth drilled, this chore was something that must be done, but Cade didn't have to like it.

The herd neared the trap where several trucks and spectators could be seen on the hill above the corrals. Cade could make out the wide girth of Billie Shining Elk.

"Is that—?" Lyn asked.

"Yes, I think so."

"Well, let him watch. He won't find anything wrong here."

Cade hoped she was right. He'd defended Lyn and the purpose of the roundup. He'd never live it down with his tribal members if one of these horses was seriously injured or died.

The mustangs swerved in an effort to avoid the area inhabited by people, prompting the pilot to dip closer into the horses' comfort zone. This spurred the mustangs to stampede toward the mouth of the trap where walls of burlap mesh had been attached to T posts. The solid cloth provided a calming effect on the running animals, blocking their view of possible escape routes, vehicles and people who might spook them into scattering. Signs of panic would be punctuated by wild running and self-destructive behavior. Fear would cause the horses to turn back, and the gathering process would need to be repeated—which wouldn't do the tired mustangs any good.

But that didn't happen. Not this time.

The burlap walls directed the horses uphill into the wings of the main enclosure. Rather than stampeding the wild horses for hours to the corral, the contractor had set the apparatus up closer to the mustangs. That meant less wear and tear on the horses, which brought Cade a measure of relief.

Water and hay had been included within the holding pens, along with gates and alleys for working and sorting the animals. The steeper grade of the path slowed the horses as they entered the alley leading to the capture pens. The contractor had set up the pens just over the opposite side of the hill so the horses wouldn't see them until it was too late. That meant the mustangs wouldn't flee and have to be gathered a second time.

A white stock trailer had arrived at six that morning for transporting the captured mustangs to a holding facility near Reno. Two volunteer veterinarians and eight BLM, Forest Service and contract personnel bustled around the system of holding pens…until the horses came into view. Then they all stooped behind the burlap walls so the mustangs wouldn't see them and bolt.

Near the entrance of the corral, a contractor crouched low, holding the halter of a pilot horse. All was ready.

"They're almost inside," Lyn said.

The horses sprinted across the valley, the chopper in hot pursuit, controlling the mustangs' movements to keep them from turning back. A melee of muscle, steel and dust.

A mare broke off from the rest of the herd, falling behind. The chopper let her go, focused on the main herd, not wanting to lose the band. The mare turned back the way she'd come, staggered, then stood with her head down, blowing hard. Too winded to go on.

"That one will be for us," Lyn said.

Yes. Provide care and retrieve any stragglers who couldn't keep up with the main herd.

Billows of dust and gravel from the rotor wash struck the horses and wranglers hidden behind the burlap. Some men tugged bandannas high over their mouths and noses.

A blast of static came from Lyn's hand radio.

"We got a mare fallen behind," the pilot warned.

Lyn lifted the radio to her mouth and pressed the talk button. "Affirmative. We see her."

But still Lyn waited, not seeming in any hurry to go after the winded horse.

"What are we waiting for?" Cade asked.

Lyn barely glanced his way. "If we ride in too soon, the mare will run again, even though she's all played out. She's frightened and alone. Possibly sick. I want to give her time to recover so we don't end up with a dead horse on our hands."

Now why hadn't he thought of that? Lyn's insight continued to surprise him.

As the mustangs entered the mouth of the trap, Beeswax bolted to the left, wheeled around and fled. He was probably trap savvy, which might account for his nervous, watchful manners.

At the top of the hill leading into the trap, a wrangler released the pilot horse and the stocky gelding ran in front of the band. The mares and foals hurried safely down into the corral. Two BLM employees jumped up from their hiding places and hurried to close the gate behind the mustangs.

Then the men backed off, giving the horses several minutes to catch their breath. Their sweat-dampened bodies steamed as they milled around the enclosure, but most of them began to settle down. Lyn gasped when the large blue roan stallion smashed his weight against the metal corral, fighting to break free.

"No, Brutus. Don't struggle, boy. You'll just hurt yourself," Lyn whispered beneath her breath.

Brutus screamed in fury, and Beeswax responded in kind. Cade hadn't recognized the stallions, but Lyn had. She knew all these horses by heart.

Beeswax stood off a safe distance away, head up as he watched his family's capture. Calling to them. Stomping his hooves with impatience. Frustrated by his lack of control. Cade felt sorry for him. The stallion's instinctual duty to protect his band had kicked into high gear, yet the stud could do nothing to save his mares.

Likewise, Brutus fought his captivity. Twice more, he slammed against the tall fence. The crashing sound stirred up the mares around him as they scurried to get out of his way. The men backed off, letting the stud cool down. Giving all the horses some space so they would relax.

Cade held his breath, hoping Brutus didn't injure himself. In their fight for freedom, many horses broke their own necks. Thankfully, the holding pen provided enough room for the horses to move and avoid fighting. Especially since this was a mixed band.

After a time, Brutus settled down, lulled by the nearness of his mares. But not Beeswax. He continued to pace the outskirts of the trap, head held

high, mane and tail flying in the wind as he trotted back and forth.

Then the sorting began. Shaking sticks with
white plastic bags taped to the end, the wranglers
shied the horses into separate pens. The men moved
the mustangs with the aid of a veterinarian. Brutus
in one pen, dry mares in another, and mares with
foals in a third. The vet "mouthed" each horse, lifting their upper lips to check their teeth and determine the age of each animal. Though Cade knew
the wranglers had a cattle prod handy in case of
a serious emergency, it was never used. Not even
on Brutus.

"Time for us to go." Radio in hand, Lyn tapped
her booted heels against Apple's sides.

The horse hurried into a gallop toward the
winded mare left behind by the rest of the herd.
Cade rode beside Lyn, his hands sheathed with
leather gloves as he clutched a lasso tightly with
his fingers. Grandfather had taught him to tag a
calf. As they neared the wild mare, he whipped the
rope high in a wide arc.

The mare saw them coming and snorted. With
wild eyes, she turned and tried to run, stumbled
and stopped. The rope whizzed overhead. Cade
threw the lasso. It slid over the mustang's ears, and
he tightened it around her damp neck before wrapping one end around the saddle horn. She jerked
back, but didn't flee. Too exhausted to run. Caught.

"She has a club foot," Lyn observed.

"She sure does, but not too deformed. It's a wonder she was able to keep up with the rest of the herd for so long." He drew in the length of rope, leading the limping mare at a tranquil pace back to the trap. Listening to her whooshing breath and seeing her head down as she plodded along in submission tore at Cade's heart. Because of her bad hoof, the vets might decide to euthanize her.

Unless Cade intervened. And right then and there, he decided to adopt the horse. With a club foot, she couldn't be ridden much, except on calm walks around the corrals back at Sunrise Ranch. But the horse would bring Kristen a lot of joy. The girl had a tender heart and would love and care for the mare. Of that, Cade had no doubt.

"She's got fire, but I doubt she'll be of much use for riding," Lyn said.

Cade disagreed. "Not for lots of running, but she'll do fine for walking. I'm gonna buy her."

Lyn snapped her head around and stared at him. "Why would you do that?"

"She's lame, just like Kristen and Matt, but her life doesn't have to be over with. She's young and can't be ridden fast, but she'll be a good, calm horse for walking young amputee kids around my corral."

She tilted her head, her eyes narrowing beneath the brim of her hat. "What are you suggesting?"

"Nothing, yet. We'll see."

But he couldn't stop thinking about the multitude of papers he'd sent in several weeks ago to see about a possible grant to start up an equine camp for amputee kids. Lyn had put the idea into his head. Nothing might come of it, but he wanted to try.

Back at the trap, Cade helped Lyn with the sorting. The transport trailer backed its wheels into two trenches they'd dug down about one foot so the horses wouldn't need to step up into the confines of the enclosure.

As they worked, the helicopter flew off to find more mustangs. By late afternoon they'd gathered a total of thirty-seven horses, and the chopper came in for basic maintenance and refueling. Not bad for a day of hard work. Over the next few weeks, they'd repeat this process until they'd rounded up enough horses to satisfy the grazing needs for this area.

The mustangs were loaded into the transport trailer, ready to go. Cade lifted his gaze to the horizon where Beeswax continued to circle the perimeter. With not a single member of his herd left behind, he was still agitated.

All alone.

Cade didn't want to feel sentimental over a wild mustang, but he thought about what he'd do if Lyn and Kristen were taken from him. He'd search for them as long as it took. He'd never give up. Never quit.

"Wait!" Lyn called as the men lifted the gate to close up the transport.

They paused, their eyes filled with irritation at this delay. They'd all worked hard and wanted to get home to evening supper.

"Let's turn one of those young mares loose," she said.

Frank Whitcomb, the man in charge from the BLM, squinted with curiosity. "What for?"

She gestured toward Beeswax. "You're taking his entire family. Give him one of the mares so he won't be out here all alone."

Cade stared at her, along with everyone else. Again, her empathy stunned him. He'd felt bad for Beeswax, but it never occurred to him to free one of the mares. Lyn's compassion touched Cade's heart like nothing else could.

"But we just caught these horses," one wrangler argued.

"Releasing one mare won't hurt anything," she insisted.

Frank hesitated, and Cade thought he might refuse Lyn. Which wouldn't be a wise choice. Lyn's jaw hardened like granite, her brown eyes darkening and becoming as sharp as flinty chips of steel. As the forest ranger and the only woman on this roundup, she'd worked as hard as the men and had earned their respect.

"You're right." Frank waved a hand for one of the men to free a horse.

A wrangler separated out a healthy mare and shooed her past the tailgate. The horse's unshod hooves pounded against the trailer floor as she backed out onto solid ground. The wranglers moved away, and the mare stood eyeing them in confusion for several moments. Then, realizing she was free, she kicked up clods of dirt and raced straight for Beeswax. The stallion called a greeting and galloped out to meet her. The two animals snorted, nudged noses and breathed each other in.

The sweetest family reunion Cade ever saw.

The transport started down the road, leaving several of the wranglers behind to clean up the trap area. It didn't take long. While Lyn helped gather up the burlap fencing, Cade rode out to retrieve several white-flag markers. Moving Flash at a slow lope, Cade rode over a low hill. His stomach rumbled with hunger. Maybe he'd invite Lyn over for a warm, home-cooked meal at his place. Dal had promised to barbecue rib-eye steaks with potatoes and salad.

Cade's mouth watered at the thought. He wasn't paying attention.

A barbed wire fence cut across the side of the embankment. Out of his peripheral vision, Cade caught a flurry of movement and jerked his head around. A rattlesnake lay half-coiled as he sunned himself on a flat stone.

Flash swerved sharply to avoid crashing over the reptile. The unexpected jostling took Cade unaware. The reins jerked from his fingers. He clutched at empty air, falling backward over the horse's rump. The ground slammed up to meet him. Pain sliced through him as his back landed on the barbed wire. Caught in the stirrup, his right leg jerked hard, then snapped. A bolt of pain shot through him. The sickening sound of his bone breaking brought a flash of bright stars across his eyes and he blinked.

Flash screamed in fear. Bowing his head, the horse humped his back and bucked. Once. Twice— Wrenching a piercing scream from Cade's throat each time.

Then all went still.

A black void clawed at Cade's mind, but he fought it off. Semiconscious, he knew his foot was still caught in the stirrup. He had to get it loose. If Flash took off at a run, he'd be dragged to his death.

He reached out a hand toward his leg, then lay there for several moments, dazed and hurting. Gasping for breath. Trying to get his bearings. Trying to stay awake.

A faint hissing sounded to his left and behind

him. The sound ebbed and faded as the snake slithered away into the shadowed underbrush.

Cade couldn't pass out. He couldn't die. Lyn and Kristen needed him, whether Lyn realized it or not. As much as he needed them. He couldn't lose them. Not now. Not like this.

So he prayed.

Lyn closed the corral gate and secured the latch. Releasing a sigh, she leaned against the iron panels for several moments, her arms and legs weighted by fatigue. She'd earned her weariness today. They'd had a successful roundup with no losses or injured horses. That pleased her immensely.

Turning, she surveyed the empty valley. Where was Cade? He should be back by now.

Dust sifted over the dirt road, heralding the passing of the transport trailer and other trucks. She and Cade were the last to leave. Since she'd picked him and Flash up early that morning, she knew he wouldn't have left with someone else. Not without telling her.

Would he?

Taking hold of the reins, she stepped up onto Apple. The leather saddle creaked as she set her feet in the stirrups. She clicked her heels against the horse's sides and loped into the valley, heading in the direction where she'd last seen Cade. Anticipating his friendly smile, she was tempted to invite him over for dinner with her and Kristen tomorrow night.

What could it hurt?

Funny how comfortable she'd become with him. How he settled her nerves without saying a single word. Just being near Cade brought her peace.

As she reached the sloping hills, she gazed down into the canyon. Nothing. No sign of him or his horse—

Wait! Flash stood several hundred feet away, his reins trailing on the ground. But where was Cade?

Riding in that direction, Lyn caught a sound. Subtle at first, then more plaintive. A croaking cry for help.

"Haw!" She urged Apple into a run.

A movement lower to the ground caught her eye. Cade! Strung up in the barbed wire, his right leg held at an odd angle, his foot still caught in the stirrup.

Broken. Lyn had no doubt.

Several yards away, she slowed Apple to a walk, endeavoring not to spook Flash into running. Her gaze took in Cade's predicament. Both arms were wrapped around barbed wire. His chambray shirt was tattered and bloodied, and his leather gloves provided little protection against the slicing barbs. But that wasn't what alarmed her. Cade lay with his head tilted back, his corded throat exposed to a sharp length of barbed wire. If Flash bolted, the man's throat would be sliced open.

"Whoa," she said gently to Flash, sliding off Apple in a slow movement.

Flash stomped one hoof and waved his head. His tail swished at a fly, but he didn't move. Thank goodness he knew Lyn well and didn't shy away.

She walked to the horse, extending an arm. She clasped the drooping reins, then held tight.

"Cade, can you hear me?"

No response, but his head rolled to the side. His eyes were closed, his dark lashes stark against his pale face.

Lyn turned Flash and tied the horse to a fence post, then gently disengaged Cade's foot from the stirrup. As she set his leg on the ground, a cry of pain wrenched from his throat.

Reaching for her radio, she called Frank, hoping he wasn't too far out of range. Praying she could get help.

"This is Frank." A burst of static followed.

"Frank, we've got an emergency. Cade's down, badly injured. Need help now."

Static squawked through the air. "Affirmative. We're on our way back. See you in twenty minutes."

Relieved to have someone coming to assist in getting Cade to a hospital, she reached into her saddlebags and pulled out a bottle of water and a bandanna. She knelt beside him, her hands trembling. She fought off the shock and fear, doing what needed to be done right now. She could fall to pieces later on, once Cade was safe.

Wetting the linen cloth, she pressed it against his lips and then his forehead. His eyes flickered open, and he gave her a weak smile.

"I knew you'd come."

His words turned her heart into soft mush. How had they come to depend on each other? To care so deeply?

"I think you have a broken leg, but I don't know how bad it is," she said. "Frank and his men are on their way back to help us get you out of here."

He gave a weak nod, swallowing hard. "Good. I feared you might have to put me down like we did that lame mare."

She inhaled a sharp breath. "That's not funny."

"I know. Thank goodness you found me in time."

Yes, thank the Lord.

"How do you feel?" she asked.

"Like a herd of wild mustangs just trampled over me."

She didn't laugh.

"Don't you leave me, you hear?" she ordered, praying he didn't have internal injuries. Praying he'd be okay.

"Not ever. Not if I can help it."

She plumped her jacket beneath his head and

washed the blood from his face and throat, making him as comfortable as possible. She was jittery with impatience as she waited for help to arrive. Sitting in the dirt beside Cade, she glared at the horizon, desperate for a cloud of dust or any other sign along the dirt road to show that Frank and his men were near.

"You saved my life," Cade said.

She hesitated, thinking over his words. "And you saved mine."

He blinked his lack of understanding.

"With Kristen. You brought her back to me," she explained.

He shook his head, a small movement that caused him to grimace. "No, you did that yourself, with the Lord's help."

"But you showed me the way. Did I tell you my husband was a marine before we got married? He served in the Gulf War."

Cade swallowed, his Adam's apple moving briefly. "Yeah, you told me."

"Well, he taught me to never leave a fallen man behind. So you stay with me, okay?"

A tentative smile curved his handsome lips. "Don't worry. I'm not gonna die. You're not getting rid of me that easily."

She hoped not.

"I'm sorry your husband died," he said after a moment.

"Yeah, me, too. I just wish I could tell him…" Her mind stumbled over the words she longed to say.

"What?"

"Oh, so many things."

"Such as?"

Why did Cade always push her out of her comfort zone? This time, she didn't mind as much, but he always seemed to know when she needed to talk. "Such as how sorry I am. The accident was my fault, Cade. All my fault."

"I thought it was a drunk driver's fault," he said.

"It was, but I was driving our car that night. We were laughing, and I wasn't paying attention to the road. I might have avoided the accident otherwise. If only I could go back in time—a few seconds is all I need to bring Rob back safely. I could give Kristen her leg back and everything would be okay—"

Tears burned her eyes and clogged her throat. She hadn't meant to confide in Cade. He was the only person she'd ever told her secret to. He'd become her best friend, and she loved him. She knew that now. It did no good to deny it.

He released a deep breath and reached for her hand, twining his fingers with hers. She didn't resist. She couldn't fight him anymore. Not now when she'd almost lost him for good. Life had become so precious to her. She didn't want to waste any more time on fear and regrets.

"The accident wasn't your fault, Lyn. You shouldn't blame yourself any more than Kristen should blame herself."

"I wish it were so easy."

"I know. But I've learned obstacles are meant to strengthen us, not defeat us. God wants us to have joy. Don't you think it's time to let go of your guilt?"

Lyn knew what he said was true, but for some reason forgiveness and joy were for other people, not her.

Until now. Until she found herself wanting to believe Cade's words. Longing to be happy again.

She would have said something more, but the whir of a helicopter reached her ears. Within minutes, the aircraft landed a short distance away, along with a smattering of dirt and gravel. Several men helped splint Cade's leg. Then they loaded him inside. He gritted his teeth against the pain, but didn't make a sound.

"Don't worry. I'll stay and help Lyn with your horses," Frank told Cade.

Cade nodded, his strong fingers folded around Lyn's, sending shock waves of electricity tingling up her arm. She hated to let him go. Hated to be parted from him for even a moment.

An anxious feeling blanketed her, but she didn't

feel afraid. Nor did she understand the emotions bubbling up inside of her. As though she'd just come home, safe and sound after being stranded alone in a thunderstorm.

The feelings of eternal love.

"Thank you." He held on tight, as if he didn't want to let go of her, either. But maybe that was just wishful thinking on Lyn's part.

"I'll take care of Flash and get him home safe," she promised.

"Dal's at the ranch. He'll help you. And I'll see you soon?" he asked.

A question, not a statement. Surely she didn't imagine the hopeful tint to his words.

"Of course. I'll bring Kristen, and we'll visit you as soon as we can."

Stepping back, she continued to gaze into his eyes. Their hands pulled apart, fingertips skimming, then dropping away. The door to the chopper slid closed, and still she stood there. Until her long ponytail whipped around her face as the aircraft lifted off.

Closing her eyes against the wind and grit, Lyn felt strangely tranquil. For the first time in a year, she actually felt free of resentment and hurt. Loving Cade didn't mean she had to stop loving Rob. It just meant she was ready to move on with her life and be happy.

Even though Kristen had the amputated leg,

Lyn's anger and fear had proven to be the greater handicap. Finally, because of Cade, she had the courage to let it all go. Because Cade had brought her back to the Lord.

Chapter Fourteen

Sunrise Ranch hadn't changed one bit since Lyn was here last week for Kristen's physical therapy with Magpie. But Lyn had. More than she could ever imagine.

As she parked her car in the graveled driveway, Kristen waved at Dal, who stood on the front porch with Gus. The dog padded down the steps and trotted over to greet the little girl as she opened her door, slid her legs around, braced her hands and stood.

"Hi, fella!" After Kristen found her balance, she rubbed the dog's ears.

Lyn got out and headed toward the house, able to clearly hear as Dal called to the screen door.

"You've got visitors, invalid. Come on outside."

A thud sounded from inside, and then Cade thrust the screen door open. Hobbling on crutches, he stepped out onto the wooden porch, the door clapping closed behind him.

"Cade!" Kristen shouted, and hurried toward him.

But Lyn reached him first. His gaze locked with hers. A variety of elated emotions burned through her, sizzling down to her toes.

"How are you?" she breathed out in a throaty sigh before clearing her ragged voice.

"I'm great, now that you're here."

Dal snorted, but they ignored him.

Kristen hugged the doctor tight and he spoke several words to her, but Lyn didn't hear a thing. The realization that she loved this man had created a funny sort of awareness within her. A happy buzzing inside her head. She felt light and energized. As though she could do anything.

If only he loved her, too.

"Hi, Dal!" Kristen greeted the handsome man.

He tugged gently on her ponytail. "Hi, honey."

The shrill chatter of her daughter brought Lyn out of her stupor.

"Hello, Dal," Lyn said.

He smiled in return, then glanced at Kristen. "You want to see what I taught Lightning this week?"

"Sure!" Using the handrail to support herself, the girl hopped down the steps.

As they headed toward the barn, Dal paused long enough to glance over his shoulder at Cade. "Come on, gimp. Hurry and keep up."

"Gimp! I've never insulted you like that," Cade called to his friend, then winked at Lyn.

"That's because I'm faster than you, even with one leg."

"When I get this cast off, we'll see who the faster man is," Cade promised.

Lyn just smiled, enjoying herself thoroughly. Wondering how to get the courage to tell Cade she loved him.

Rather than follow his buddy and Kristen out to the barn, Cade sat on a wicker sofa on the porch. "Will you join me for a while?"

Lyn sat next to him, feeling suddenly shy.

"I didn't mean to scare you with the accident," he said. "Thanks for coming back for me."

"You're welcome. But please don't frighten me like that ever again."

A chuckle rumbled in his wide chest. "I'll sure try not to, believe me."

A long silence followed as he took her hand in his.

"When I found you, I was so scared," she confided. "You were covered with so much blood, I didn't think you'd make it."

"I kind of scared myself."

She licked her dry lips and glanced down at the cast on his leg. The break had looked worse than it was, thank the Lord.

"But it was more than just being scared, Cade. I…I thought I might lose you. For good."

He turned to face her, his hypnotic eyes creased with wonder. "You did?"

She nodded and lifted her gaze to his. "Yes, and I didn't like it. You see, I care for you, Cade. A lot."

He swallowed, his breath leaving him in a short gasp. As if he couldn't believe what she'd said. Either that, or he didn't want to hear her words.

"I care a lot for you, too. But I'm afraid that doesn't explain my feelings well enough."

"What do you mean?" She crossed her ankles and looked away, not daring to hope. Picking a piece of lint off her summer dress.

"I love you, Lyn. More than I can ever say. I love Kristen, too. But caring for you is just the tip of the iceberg for me. I want a lot more. I want us to be a real family."

"You do?" The heat of his tall body felt warm against her side, and she brushed her damp forehead with the back of her hand.

"Uh-huh." The rough calluses on his palm slid against her hand.

"Well, I guess now is a good time to confess I feel the same. I love you, too. So very much."

Dark brows shot up, his eyes glittering with curiosity. He laughed, a low, rumbling sound that sent shock waves through Lyn's chest. "Do you know how long I've waited to hear you say that, lady?"

She shook her head, enjoying the rich timbre of his voice.

"Since the first moment I saw you standing in my clinic," he said. "I think I've loved you since I rescued you from being trampled by that wild stallion. I've just been waiting for you to let me in. To realize we should be together."

"You have?" That giddy sensation she'd felt at seeing him earlier now became a full onslaught of elation.

"Yeah, now that we've confessed we're in love, I can finally ask you out on a date." He shook his head. "We've kind of done this backward, but it's okay as long as we get there. Are you up for dinner and a movie with me tomorrow night?"

She frowned, a bit of doubt clouding her mind. "You could have any woman you want, Cade. I'm damaged goods. My life is so complicated. Why would you want Kristen and me?"

He brushed his fingertips over her cheek, making her skin tingle. "Because color flooded my life the moment I met you. No one else has ever made me feel like this before. No one else will do. Not for me. Just you and Kristen. That's all I want. Except for maybe more children in the future."

Another baby. The thought brought Lyn so much hope, she couldn't contain the joy. She hugged him—she couldn't resist. Not when he said such sweet words to her. Not when she wanted this, too.

"I also have a secret I want to share with you," he said.

Her mind spun with happiness. "What's that?"

"You remember when you proposed I buy some of the wild horses and let Dal gentle them and open a camp here at the ranch for amputee kids?"

She nodded, feeling impertinent for ever suggesting such a thing. After all, it wasn't her business what he—

"Well, I took your advice."

"You did?"

"Yeah, I researched a grant from the American Coalition for Amputees. I've applied and, with my medical contacts, it appears I'll qualify for funding a horse camp for amputee children."

"But what about starting your outfitters business?"

"That never seemed to fit, or I would have done it by now. But I think a horse camp for amputee kids would work great. I'd be near town in case someone needed a doctor. And I've got plenty of room here at the ranch. I'm gonna adopt quite a few of the younger wild horses and train them for riding. Dal says he wants to help. Of course, I haven't worked out all the logistics, but I really want to do this. With you by my side."

She stared, hardly able to believe what he said. "That's so wonderful, Cade. You're such an amazing man. I have no doubt you can do anything you set your mind to."

He lifted his arm and tightened it around her shoulders. "As long as I have you and Kristen beside me, I can do it. I know we haven't even kissed yet, but I want to be a permanent part of your and Kristen's lives. I want us to be a family for keeps."

"Oh, Cade. I can't think of anything more wonderful."

"Will you marry me, Lyn? This isn't how I planned to propose to you, but I can't wait any longer. Will you marry me and let me date you?"

She laughed around the tears spilling down her cheeks. "Yes, Cade. Nothing would make me happier. Nothing in the world."

As he pulled her close for a long kiss, she melted within his arms. She leaned against his strong shoulder and wet his neck with her tears.

This was what she wanted. For so long. Her and Kristen. And Cade.

A real family. For always. Forever.

Epilogue

The smell of dust and horses sifted over the air. The dry summer heat beat down on Lyn, forcing her to adjust the wide brim of her cowboy hat lower across her face. Squirming on the hard bench in the spectator stands, she wished they hadn't sat so close to the animal corrals. But she wanted to be near Kristen. In spite of her nauseous stomach, Lyn wouldn't miss this event for the world.

"You okay, honey?" Sitting beside her, Cade leaned in close.

Lyn breathed deeply of his light, spicy scent. His fragrance almost wiped away the hot animal smell rising from the rodeo arena below.

Almost.

With a quick nod, she held the empty popcorn container close in case she finally lost control over her queasy stomach.

"You don't look so good," he said. "Your cheeks

are flushed with heat. Maybe bringing you here today wasn't such a good idea after all."

His doubtful gaze lowered to her round stomach, where their unborn child nestled safely within her.

"I'm not leaving," she said. "Kristen's up next, and I want to see our daughter ride."

As if on cue, the announcer called the girl's name over the loudspeaker. "Kristen Warner-Baldwin is our next barrel racer in the peewee competition, folks. She's from Stokely, Nevada, and has been riding barrels just two years now."

A loud cheer rose from the stadium. If she wasn't seeing it with her own eyes, Lyn wouldn't believe her daughter could be here at the Reno rodeo, competing in the barrel races. It looked like all of them were about to reach their fondest dreams.

"You think Dal will remember to check the cinch on her saddle before he lets her ride?" Lyn asked. "Maybe you should go down and be with her. She might need your help."

Old habits died hard, and her mind still thought of everything that might go wrong. Except now she had other people to assist in making sure her child was safe.

"No, I'm right where I need to be. Dal loves that girl and knows what to do. Except for you or me, Kristen couldn't be in better hands."

He'd barely finished his words when Kristen came barreling past on a horse. Like a streak of lightning, she zoomed to the first barrel and around, tilting with her mount, as though she were one with the animal. To the next barrel and the next. Riding like a pro, her legs securely settled within the stirrups. And then the home stretch, holding out the reins to give her horse her head. The mare wasn't Lightning—rather, one of the wild horses from the roundup—but she was just as fast. Dal had trained the animal for riding, with Kristen close beside him all the way. In fact, the girl had become an amazing horsewoman.

Kristen rode the mustang at breakneck speed, and Lyn held her breath. The mare was a perfect lady for Kristen to ride until Lightning got older. But Lyn still worried about her girl. Lyn figured that worrying about her children was a mother's curse. It never went away, even when you were old and gray.

With Cade's arm securely around her back, Lyn stood and yelled her lungs out. She bounced on the bleachers, her nausea completely forgotten. And when the broadcaster announced Kristen's time, the spectators roared.

Second place. It wasn't first, but second place was just as good to Lyn. No one knew Kristen was an amputee kid. She'd forbidden her family from telling anyone. But Lyn knew everything her girl had overcome, everything she'd done to be just another normal child.

Glancing down, Lyn saw Dal sitting high on one of the corral gates. He pushed his cowboy hat back and gave them a thumbs-up, a wide grin beaming on his face. Lyn and Cade waved their approval.

"Our girl's done well today," Cade said.

"Yes, she has."

Our girl. After almost two years of marriage, Lyn couldn't think of a better way to put it. With another child on the way and Cade's horse camp for amputee children off and running, she couldn't imagine a more complete, happy life. Her work with the wild horses and the Toyakoi Shoshone Tribe continued. The answers weren't easy, but she never gave up the battle to try to protect the mustangs and do what she believed was right.

Stepping up on her tiptoes, she pressed a warm kiss against Cade's lips. He smiled and kissed her again, holding her tight in front of anyone who chose to look.

"What was that for?" he asked, gazing down into her eyes with a delighted grin.

"Just because I love you, sweetheart. Just because you're mine."

Again he kissed her, a lingering show of affection she wished could go on forever. After all, he was her husband and they were about to have their second child. They'd built a life together. They were happy.

His hand slid over her tight baby tummy. "And I love you, honey. I always will."

"That's all I need to hear." She breathed the words in a breathless sigh.

"Come on. Let's go congratulate our daughter. We're going out to dinner tonight to celebrate."

"And then we're gonna find Dal a nice woman to date. He needs to get married and settle down, too."

Cade frowned. "He does?"

She nodded. "Definitely. He's too good a man to not have a family of his own."

Cade chuckled. "Poor Dal. I doubt he's ready for your matchmaking."

As Cade took Lyn's hand firmly in his and led the way, the peace and contentment she'd longed for rested on her heart like the hand of God. She owed the Lord so much. She owed Him everything. With a fulfilling career and a family to cherish, she could ask for nothing more.

* * * * *

If you enjoyed this story by Leigh Bale,
be sure to check out the other books this month
from Love Inspired!

Dear Reader,

Have you ever been afraid? I mean, really, constantly afraid. Of everything and nothing. Living your entire life in fear that something bad might happen? And that you wouldn't be able to deal with it if it happened? Maybe bad things happened to you in the past to make you feel this way. And so it gave you a fear of bad things happening again, in the future. And that you wouldn't be able to cope with it.

All of us face discouragement in life. We know Christ was the Good Shepherd. The great example for all of us. He left the ninety-and-nine to go after the one lost lamb. Even He faced great and cruel hardships and died for us. To give us the gift of the Atonement, so that all might be saved.

In *Healing the Forest Ranger,* I've had to oversimplify a very complicated issue in dealing with the wild horses. Many mustangs are injured during roundups. Approximately one percent of them die. To gather up the horses might seem cruel. Likewise, to leave them and other wildlife to starvation is just as cruel. There are no easy answers to this problem. Both the hero and heroine are fighting to protect these animals. The problems have become almost impossible to deal with. I believe this is because we want to stop all death and suffering of any kind, and we can't. Much of it is out of our control, so we must rely on the Lord to handle the rest. The hero and heroine's methods might differ, but their goals are the same. As they try to help the wildlife in their area, they are able to heal their own broken hearts and find joy in God's redeeming love.

We all are a part of this earth and God's creations. He wants us to be happy. He is very aware of each and every one of us. Just as He went after the one lost lamb, so does He also watch over you and me. Because we live in an imperfect world, there is death and sorrow. But I believe God has given us these imperfections so that we might learn to recognize goodness and joy. There is no joy without sorrow. No health without sickness. God allows us to suffer hardships that we might not understand, but He knows it is for our betterment and personal growth. He is the great equalizer. In Him, all things will be renewed. Every plant and creature upon the earth may be fully restored.

I hope you've enjoyed reading *Healing the Forest Ranger,* and I invite you to visit my website at www.LeighBale.com to learn more about my books.

May you find peace in the Lord's words!

Leigh Bale

Questions for Discussion

1. In *Healing the Forest Ranger,* Lyndsy Warner is a forest ranger who lost her husband in a horrible car crash that also took her daughter's leg. Though Lyn suffered very little injury, she bears horrible scars on the inside due to guilt for surviving unscathed. Have you or someone you love ever suffered some kind of trauma that left them scarred on the inside? How did you or your loved one deal with it? Was it easy to get over, or did it take a long time? Why do you think some people are able to heal from mental trauma faster than others?

2. Dr. Cade Baldwin is a former U.S. marine, now a doctor, who still suffers from post-traumatic stress disorder. He's been able to cope with occasional moments of panic by focusing on the Lord. Do you think everyone can deal with all their problems in such a way, or do you think some people might also need psychological help from a skilled doctor to overcome their trauma? Why or why not?

3. Kristen, Lyn's ten-year-old daughter, had an amputation above her right knee. When Cade Baldwin first starts working with the girl to help improve her walking, he tries to teach

her to trust her prosthesis to be there and support her weight whenever she steps forward. At first, this is hard for Kristen, but over time she learns to trust and is able to walk and run without a limp. How can we liken this process to trusting our Heavenly Father to be there for us whenever we need Him? Have you ever operated your life on pure faith in God? Were you afraid? Was it easy for you to cast aside your doubts? Why or why not?

4. Because of all they have lost in the past, Lyn is highly overprotective of Kristen and refuses to let the girl play soccer or ride a horse. Do you think Lyn is wise in this decision? Why or why not?

5. Fear has become a constant companion of Lyn's. Many people fear they won't have enough money, that they aren't good enough, what others might think of them, that they'll lose their house or that someone they love might die, etc. Have you ever lived in constant fear over something bad happening? Or is there someone you know who lives this way? How can prayer and faith in God help us overcome living in fear?

6. Over time, Lyn comes to realize her fear and overprotectiveness is destroying her relation-

ship with her daughter and stifling Kristen. Have you ever struggled with being too protective of someone else? How might this attitude damage their self-reliance and inner confidence? Do you believe it's best to always step in and help others? What is the fine line to determine when to help and when to stand back and let others do what they can for themselves? Have you met people who tend to always want you to do things for them rather than doing it themselves? How can you help them recognize that they might be happier if they are able to do things without help? (Note: I realize there are no easy answers to these questions.)

7. Lyn is a forest ranger and must concern herself with all the wildlife living within the ranger district she presides over. Cade is a wild-horse advocate who believes the mustangs should be left alone to run wild on the range, where they have lived for centuries. This is a highly emotional issue for many people, but Lyn and Cade try to work together to understand the various issues and to find a resolution that will work well for each entity concerned. Do you think this is a wise practice? Why or why not?

8. Just as Lyn must trust Cade to provide the best medical care for her daughter, Cade must trust

Lyn to do what is right for the wild horses. Have you ever had to rely on someone you didn't want to trust? And vice versa? How did you handle the situation? Did it have a positive outcome? Why or why not?

9. Neither Lyn nor Cade ever plan to become friends, but after saving a wild foal and sharing some other unusual experiences together, they can't help caring for each other as more than just acquaintances. Have you ever become friends with someone you planned not to like? What preconceived notions or biases kept you from liking this person in the beginning? What changed your mind later on? Do you think it's fair to decide not to like a person without first knowing them? Why or why not?

10. When Lyn goes with Cade up into the mountains to check on the wild horses, she points out some desert flowers to him. Though Cade has lived in this area all his life, he's never noticed such things before. Likewise, Lyn teaches Cade to think about even the lowly snakes and rodents. Have you ever heard the expression that we should "stop and smell the roses"? What do you think that really means? Have you ever overlooked the beauty of God's creations and then noticed them later on? Why do you think

people tend to do this now and then? What do you think we can do to be more aware of the magnificent world around us? Do you think there is a beauty to reptiles and small mammals? What about insects? Why do you think all of these creatures are important to the earth?

11. When Cade and Lyn find the wild mare with the compound fracture, he decides to shoot the horse as a mercy and put her out of her misery. Considering how much he loves the wild mustangs and what he suffered during war, this is especially difficult for Cade. Have you or someone close to you ever been forced to destroy something you loved? Did you consult God about it beforehand? How did you recover from the ordeal?

12. Cade wants to prevent a roundup of the wild horses if at all possible. Lyn is convinced a roundup is the most humane way to help the mustangs and other wildlife in the area. This difference of opinion almost destroys Cade and Lyn's romantic relationship, until Cade realizes nothing is more important to him than being with Lyn and her young daughter. Do you think Cade made the right decision? Why or why not?

13. Have you ever broken off a romantic relationship with someone because you disagreed over something that was highly important to you? Do you think it's possible for two people who are in love to "agree to disagree" on important issues and share a respectful and fulfilling relationship in spite of their disagreement? Why or why not?

LARGER-PRINT BOOKS!

GET 2 FREE LARGER-PRINT NOVELS PLUS 2 FREE MYSTERY GIFTS

Love Inspired

Larger-print novels are now available...

LILPDIR13R

LARGER-PRINT BOOKS!

GET 2 FREE
LARGER-PRINT NOVELS
PLUS 2 FREE
MYSTERY GIFTS

Love Inspired®

SUSPENSE
RIVETING INSPIRATIONAL ROMANCE

Larger-print novels are now available...

LISLPDIR13R

ReaderService.com

Manage your account online!

- Review your order history
- Manage your payments
- Update your address

We've designed the Harlequin® Reader Service website just for you.

Enjoy all the features!

- Reader excerpts from any series
- Respond to mailings and special monthly offers
- Discover new series available to you
- Browse the Bonus Bucks catalog
- Share your feedback

Visit us at:

ReaderService.com